UNLAWFUL PASSAGE

UNLAWFUL PASSAGE

RISE OF MAGIC BOOK 5

CM RAYMOND   LE BARBANT   MICHAEL ANDERLE

DISRUPTIVE IMAGINATION

MAP

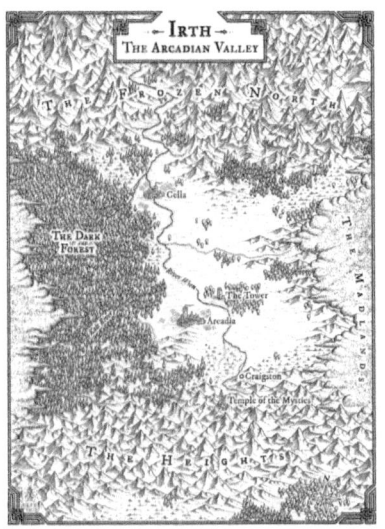

CHAPTER ONE

From their altitude, the strip of land dividing the two massive bodies of water appeared the size of Hannah's middle finger. She laughed as the wind whipped through her hair and Sal's scales rubbed against her thighs as she gripped him for dear life.

Between Hannah and the foreign ground below, floated the airship, which looked like a child's toy from their altitude. They had been flying east on the ship, which Parker had taken to calling the *Unlawful*, for days on end. Ezekiel, as curious and coy as ever, had asked her and her friends to join him on an epic quest to save the Oracle, Lilith, and with her, all of Irth.

You know, no big deal.

She didn't know much about what was waiting for them at their destination, but so far, the epic world-saving quest had consisted mostly of watching Laurel and Karl bicker on the deck of the ship while Parker and Hadley sought to one-up each other.

Hannah had come to love their flying home, but as she and Sal soared through the spotless blue sky, she was happy to put some space between her and it—at least for a second.

Gripping harder with her legs, she reached back and pulled her hair into a ponytail, before shouting the command.

"Dive, you lazy wretch," she screamed at the dragon, her voice hardly winning over the howling air around them.

Sal tilted his head back toward Hannah, and shot his tongue out of his mouth and back in before snapping his body up toward the sun and whipping it around back toward the world below.

"Shit!" Hannah yelled as they picked up speed, plummeting downward to the strange land.

Arcadia was hundreds, if not thousands of miles behind them. Despite the fact that she had lived there her whole life, the city felt like a dream from her past.

Adrien was dead, the injustices that plagued her and her friends defeated. Hannah had assumed that once she avenged her brother, she would get a chance to relax. Live a normal life. But if the dragon under her was any indication, she would never experience anything close to normal ever again.

On days like this, she was absolutely fine with it.

As they descended, the land looked less and less like a child's drawing and more like the real world. She craned her neck as they passed the airship, but they were moving far too quickly to catch a glimpse of her friends watching them in awe from the deck.

The ground was coming fast, making her grip more tightly. With Sal's speed, she swore they could crash straight through and onto the other side.

"Sal?" she screamed, but her words were sucked out of her mouth by the wind which threatened to pull her from the dragon's back. "Sal!" she tried again.

The blur of the world beneath took on detail, and she could see the ruins of a city, a place that would have been a major point of human dwelling before the Age of Madness. She screamed again, but this time, only in her mind. She felt her creature's muscles tense in response. They were tied together, and he knew exactly what she was thinking, but he still dove.

Ruins of a tower, not unlike the one she and Ezekiel called

their own, rushed past. The windows blurred into dark lines as the ground rose up to meet them. Hannah fought the urge to close her eyes, and at the last second, Sal shifted his body—his wings grabbing at the hot air which surrounded them.

Just before the impact that would have made them both splotches of flesh and blood on the remains of the street, he pulled out of the dive and drifted lazily between the ruins of the ancient city.

Hannah's heart pounded. "Yeehaw!" she shouted into the quiet oblivion that surrounded her.

Sal slowed his flight, circled over a clearing between what remained of four ancient buildings, and settled down with a thump. His wings folded onto his back, and he glanced back at his master, beady eyes blinking in her direction.

Hannah laughed and slammed his side with an open palm. "You are one bad ass son of a bitch."

He laid his jaw on the ground, allowing her to throw her leg over his head and dismount. As her feet hit solid ground, it took a second for her head to stop swimming. Looking back at Sal, she said, "OK, enough showing off. I won't call you lazy ever again."

She surveyed his body. Once the dragon was a common newt on the streets of Arcadia, but now he had grown to the size of the biggest carts that were used to haul amphoralds into the city from the Heights. But as far as she could tell, he hadn't grown for a while. Which was good, considering their accommodations aboard the ship that once belonged to Adrien, the tyrant of Arcadia.

Maybe he had reached his peak.

Despite their closeness, there was so much she didn't know about the dragon. Zeke, the most experienced person Hannah had ever met, claimed to never have seen magic quite like it. It's part of what made Hannah so special.

She gave one more pat to Sal's side before turning her attention to the ruins which surrounded her. The broken buildings loomed skyward on every side, and she felt strangely hedged in by them. She had never seen so many artifacts from the age before. Rubble was strewn out around her, but she could almost imagine the city, built by machines in a day long forgotten.

Now, little remained of the city. But it was the silence, more so than the buildings themselves, that made her feel uneasy. It smothered her like a thick fog.

"You smell anything, boy?" she asked, glancing back at the dragon. He had already closed his eyes—and she could hear his faint snoring. In a minute, it would be a rumble. "I'll take that as a no," she said.

She turned her head back toward the airship, wondering if Ezekiel knew they had taken to the ground. He had warned her to stay in the air. Their mission was far too important to risk the dangers of the world beneath their flying fortress. But the airship was too boring. She had lived all her life in one place. To not look around seemed like a waste.

Even so, she hoped the old man was ignorant of their entrance into the city.

Before she could think about her mentor any further, a scream cut through the silence of the ruins. She jerked her head in the direction of its source as the sound reverberated around her.

Sal was awake in an instant, fully alert and staring at his master.

"Let's go," she grunted as she took off down the city street, dodging the rubble in her path. Sal followed, hot on her heels.

The scream resounded again. This time, the words were clear. "Help!" a shrill, high voice exclaimed.

Hannah picked up the pace as the rhythm of her heart followed suit. She knew it was risky, but no way in hell was she going to ignore a cry for help. It wasn't in her nature.

Reaching the end of the corridor, dwarfed by the ruins rising above her, she cut to the right, down a side street. As she turned the corner, she found a group of four men, taller than the tallest Arcadian, circled around a cloaked figured trembling on the ground.

Memories rushed back—of the Hunters who had nearly taken her life on the day she first felt her magic. Once again, her power boiled with her rage beneath her skin.

"Get away from the kid!" she screamed in their direction.

They turned, eyes wide, as they looked with curiosity at the strange girl standing before them. A smile cracked the lead man's face when he realized they would have a grown woman to play with along with the child at their feet. But his smile melted as his eyes found Sal standing behind her.

"The hell is that?" he grunted, pointing a makeshift club at the dragon.

Hannah tilted her head and smiled. "Every girl needs a pet. Mine would just rather rip your balls off than shake hands." Hannah glanced back at Sal, who was crouched ready for attack. The normally calm animal was a ball of rage.

She held up her palm in his direction but spoke to the goons. "I'll give you one chance to get the hell out of here and never come back."

The men laughed. Another with a bald head covered in body art grinned. "Honey, I ain't afraid of no lizard. I've got balls of steel and a dick made of iron." He stepped forward away from the others. Reaching down, he grabbed his crotch and gyrated his hips. "Maybe you'd like to shake hands?"

Hannah arced her arms across her chest, pulling two perfectly round fireballs into existence. "Sorry, doucher. I'm saving myself for a human."

His mouth dropped open as she launched the fireballs, which landed square on his chest, knocking the man back into a sizzling pile of flesh.

A grin formed on Hannah's face. "Who's next?"

Without warning, the other three charged. Hannah cut to her

right, toward the largest of the three. She dropped as he approached. Pulling her silver dagger from her belt, she rolled under his attack, slicing his hamstring on her way. The man screamed in rage and pain as he dropped to the ground. Spinning back toward him, she pulled the dagger across his throat, cutting his cries of agony short.

She looked up, just in time to see Sal pivot, knocking one of the remaining men with his spiked tail into the ruins with a crash just before he leapt onto the other, ripping at exposed flesh with his dagger-sharp teeth.

Getting up from the rubble, the other man shook off the dust and gritted his teeth. "Who the hell are you? Where are you from?"

"I'm Hannah, from Arcadia."

"Arcadia? Never heard of it," the man grimaced as he pulled a weapon from his hip. "You're gonna wish you stayed there, bitch."

Hannah held her knife out toward him. "Where I'm from, that's no way to talk to a girl. Unless, of course, she's the Queen Bitch."

He held his weapon, which looked like a simple billy club, in front of him. With a grin, he pulled out a long double-edged blade. It was a handsome weapon, but there was no time for admiration. The man sprinted with a scream, swinging the sword as he approached.

Hannah held her ground.

The man swung the blade at her head, but just when it should have met its target, the weapon sliced through thin air.

He staggered forward, unable to understand the illusion her mental magic played on him.

"Never call a magician a bitch," Hannah said as she reappeared behind him.

She drew the power of present anger and past rage through her body and allowed it to exit through her open palms.

The man didn't have a chance to turn and face the one who ended his miserable life.

"Ho-lee-shite," a small voice said from behind her.

She spun, ready for attack, but dropped her hands to her side as she looked into the big, blue eyes of the boy.

———

Parker leaned against the railing on the bow of the ship laughing as he watched Hannah and Sal sail past in a blur. "She's going to kill her-damned-self one of these days," he said, shaking his head as he watched his friend and her dragon get smaller and smaller until they blended into the ground beneath.

Sipping his tea, Hadley laughed. "What she's been through? I imagine it's going to take something stronger than a fall from a thousand feet to finish her off."

The men grew quiet for a moment as they watched the landscape float lazily by. Parker had lost count of the days, and even weeks they had been airborne on Adrien's flying machine—the ship that now belonged to him and his friends—but he knew it had been too long. Quarters were getting tight, and he and the rest of the crew were getting anxious to walk on solid ground. Everyone except Hadley, that is.

Parker tilted his head toward his friend. "You really don't mind it up here, do you?"

"Mind? After all those weeks in the lowlands and cooped up in Arcadia and then that tower, I'm happy to have open air around me." Hadley grinned, his eyes surveying billowing clouds on the horizon and the mountains rising up toward their ship. "Figure this is the closest thing I'm going to get to the Heights for some time."

"Maybe ever," Parker said, raising a brow.

"Like hell. I'll get home eventually. It's been good to be out of the mountains, stretch my legs a bit—meet some peculiar folk—

but like any mystic on pilgrimage, the temple is where we belong."

Parker let the quiet take over again. His friend had a point. When they weren't below, everyone running into each other, things could be quite peaceful on the deck. The winter of the revolution was slipping into spring, and the world was coming alive once again. And he had a thousand-foot view of it all. Still, after all the running around it took to take down Adrien, the peace was downright boring.

He glanced back, looking down the length of the ship and off its stern. Arcadia was hundreds of miles behind him, and the revolution seemed like a lifetime ago. But the Founder had a new quest for them, and Hannah was committed to seeing it finished. Which meant Parker was committed as well.

Turning his head back over the bow's railing, he asked, "You think the old man is insane?"

"Ezekiel?" Hadley cocked his head like a dog in thought. "Sure. I mean most of the masters are. All that power coursing through them, it's a wonder they can stand upright. Wouldn't say it to her face, but Julianne got a crack or two with the crazy stick as well. Probably why it was her that was chosen to lead the mystics instead of me."

"I'm sure talent—or in your case, lack thereof—had nothing to do with it."

Hadley faced Parker as his eyes flashed white. The edges of his mouth turned up. "It's OK, mate. You don't need to be intimidated by me. Not everyone can have a mind like mine… But still, there's no need for low blows."

Parker laughed. "Get the hell out of my head, you freak."

"Better yours than Hannah's. All she thinks about is sex and justice."

"Yeah, well, she—wait," Parker said, suddenly standing straight up. "What's that about sex?"

"Nevermind…" Hadley let the word trail behind him as he turned and left Parker alone on the bow of the ship.

He knew the mystic was screwing with him, at least he assumed so. From what he could tell, Hadley had little chance of getting into her head. Hannah grew stronger every day, and with each sunrise, his childhood friend was more and more capable of directing the tremendous power that flowed through her own blood—giving her greater and greater defense against the mystic's tinkering.

But Parker still wondered if his handsome friend shared his desires for the young magician—and to what extent Hannah reciprocated them. Most of Hadley's comments seemed in jest, but he knew none should underestimate the mind games of a mystic—friend or not.

Eyes darting, he scanned the sky looking for Hannah and Sal to return.

"Stay out of trouble, Hannah," he whispered into the wind.

The kid reached down and grabbed a rock, which barely fit in his palm.

Hannah raised her hands in response. "Easy, there, tiger. I just saved your ass. Seems a rock to the face isn't any way to say thank you." She smiled as Sal ambled up next to her, crouched at her side, and leaned his head against her leg. "What's your name?"

The boy's eyes cut to the dragon; he stared without blinking. "Seriously, what is that?"

Sal pawed at the ground, waiting for his master to respond. As far as Hannah could tell, the dragon understood the human tongue. If nothing else, he always responded appropriately.

Reaching down to scratch his chin, she said, "Not a *that*. Sal's a *he*. Well, usually he acts like one. His name is Sal, and he's my dragon."

Sal looked up, tilted his head, and whipped his forked tongue out of his mouth and back in.

Hannah giggled. "And... I guess I better say that I'm his human, before I piss him off." Hannah lowered her voice. "For seeming so badass, I think he has a bit of a self-esteem issue."

The boy finally cracked a smile. "So, he's safe then?"

"No way. Not safe in the least. But he's mine, and... I'm his. So, as long as you drop that rock and behave yourself, he'll be safe enough for you." She watched the rock leave the kid's hand and rattle to the ground. "Now, back to my question. You got a name?"

"Hasan," he said with some hesitation. The boy glanced over his shoulder at the closest alleyway, which was littered by the rubble from the crumbling buildings that rose around it. He looked back at the dragon and then back to Hannah. "It means handsome, at least that's what my ma tells me."

Hannah's face warmed, thinking of her own mother. She would have told Hannah and Will anything to make them feel prouder than they had the day before, so she could understand the boy's blush. "Well, your mother is a keen woman. I'm sure you'll be a lady killer someday soon." She winked as he grew a darker shade of red. Hannah motioned around her. "What is this place, Hasan?"

"This place? What do you mean?"

"You know, where the hell are we?"

His brow furrowed, and his nose scrunched as he tried to make sense of the question. "It's where you are. How do you not know where it is?"

Hannah realized the boy's world, like so many in Irth, was minute. She assumed he lacked the imagination able to conceive of places days away—let alone weeks. Before meeting Ezekiel, she wasn't so different than him.

She pointed into the sky at the airship hovering overhead.

From the distance, it looked like little more than a dot floating in place. "That's my airship."

"Dragons and airships… *Kasar*, what's next?"

Hannah assumed that the foreign word was akin to the rearick's *'scheisse'*, and she was correct. "There are many and stranger things out there, man. But, for now, that ship has brought me from a city a long way from here called Arcadia. This place, your place, is a land that I know nothing about."

The boy snorted. "Not my place." He nodded toward the bodies of the men Hannah had ended. "Guess it's theirs more than anyone's. I just come to scavenge. We, my ma and me, live beyond the ruins. But this place is Constantine's." He said it like she should know who Constantine was.

She didn't. "Who's Constantine?"

The boy giggled again, enjoying the ignorance shared between them. "Hell if I know, lady. I'm not even sure if there is a Constantine. It's just what everybody calls this place. If there is a guy, I never met him." Hasan pushed his sleeve across his forehead, wiping away a mix of sweat and dirt. He looked up and gauged the position of the sun. "I need to get going. My ma is going to freak if I don't get back soon. She's nervous, lost a lot."

Hannah nodded and extended her hand. The boy took it and feigned a man's grip. "My name's Hannah. It is a pleasure to meet you, Hasan. Doubt our paths will cross again, but if they do…"

"I'll be sure to save your ass next time," he said with a smile. "And—thanks, Hannah." He looked down at the dragon by her side. "You, too, Sal."

The kid turned and ran for the alley closest to them, leaping over rocks and scurrying out of sight.

Hannah patted Sal on the side as she surveyed the bodies in the street. "Nice work, you lazy bag of scales."

After collecting their weapons, she swung a leg over Sal's spiked back and gave him a kick. He responded, wings flapping with intention as he pulled them toward the floating airship.

CHAPTER TWO

Sal slid to a stop on the deck of the ship with Hannah holding on for dear life to his neck. The momentum nearly sent her swimming in the air overboard.

"Nice landing," Parker said with a grin.

"Don't listen to his shit, Sal." She patted him on the side before whispering, "But yes, let's work on that, you clumsy lizard."

In response, Sal twisted his shoulders, sending Hannah rolling off onto the deck. She looked back at him and grinned. She usually had the last laugh, this time it belonged to the dragon.

"Where the hell you been, anyway?" Parker asked, crossing the deck to join his friend. His words were curt, but he pulled her into a warm hug that showed his concern. "I was worried."

Hannah wanted him to hold her like that forever, but she saw Hadley looking on, and Karl across the ship from where they stood. She pushed him away. "Oh, you know. Just down there saving the helpless from asshats of all kinds. It's kinda my thing."

Joining them, Hadley gave her a nod. "Welcome home, Hannah. The ship felt far too big without you, which is saying a lot since we're still all stacked on top of each other here." He turned to the Sal. "And you... I know you've been flapping those wings pretty hard, and by the looks of the blood in your claws, you've engaged in some extracurricular activities. You didn't happen to bring us back a deer or some lamb, did you?"

Hannah shrugged. "You do *not* want to eat what Sal killed. Trust me. Unless you've learned a thing or two about fine dining from the remnant."

Hadley grimaced. "I'd like to think I'm an openminded kind of guy, but I draw the line at roasted asshat. Although, I can't speak for our master chef. We're going to need some food up here quick before the rearick starts choosing which one of us he's going to roast over an open flame."

Karl, who had been leaning over the railing since they'd returned, glanced over his shoulder. His face was greener than the pines surrounding the tower. "Don't talk about food, lad. If that damned fool below won't learn to fly this thing straight, I'm gonna keep losin' my lunch over the side, and I'll be as skinny as the blasted druid before ya know it."

They all laughed at Karl's expense. None of them took to the air as well as they'd hoped, except for Hadley. He loved being in the clouds. The rest of them spent much of the days trying to get their airlegs under them. But Karl, whose long life was spent on solid ground, was having the hardest time of them all.

Giving Hadley a nod, Hannah turned to Sal. "You heard him, bud. We're going to need you to go find us some game, OK?" He nodded at his master. "And no more squirrels; it's far too disturbing for Laurel and her little friend."

Before she could say anything else, Sal took three strides and dove over the rail. She smiled as she watched him go. Sal had been invaluable to them, and hunting was the least of what he brought to the team.

The airship suddenly lurched, forcing everyone to grab ahold of something. Karl's face disappeared over the edge of the ship again, along with what little he had managed to eat that day.

"Don't worry, Karl," Hannah said with a grin. "I'm sure your stomach will catch up with us eventually."

"Screw you, lassie. One more jolt like that, and I'm gonna throw that damned kid overboard."

"Careful," she said. "Gregory's all we've got to fly this thing. Hell if any of the rest of us know how to move this freighter. All we're good at is cursing and fighting."

"What else do ya need?" Karl asked as he composed himself. "And I say just crash this damned heap. We'll let 'er burn on the ground and walk our asses all the way to the wizard's friends. Scheisse, a few miles on the old boots would be a shit ton less torturous than this."

Hannah stepped over to her friend and rubbed his shoulder. They gave each other plenty of playful words, but she cared for him more than she'd ever tell him. And even if she'd make fun of him until their dying days, she'd never think poorly of the brave rearick.

"It'll take years to walk there, at least as far as any of us know. We don't have that kind of time."

Karl pushed his sleeve across his beard, clearing away a few of the remains of breakfast he had recycled. "Aye, the Great Darkness or whatever. Like all the magical freaks I've met, Ezekiel would shave his beard before givin' a straight answer. Any chance he's given you any more clues ta what the hell we're after?"

Hannah cast her eyes to the rough boards of the deck. She wished she had an answer for Karl, for all of them. But she didn't. Though not all magicians were guilty of the rearick's charges, many were obtuse, and Ezekiel was the greatest among them. But since the time she had started her training, nearly a year prior, she had learned that getting Ezekiel to talk before he was ready was like trying to make a kettle boil before its time.

"Wish I knew more," she said, bringing her eyes back up to Karl's. "But we just need to trust him."

Karl laughed and snorted, "If I didn't trust him, I wouldn't be on this damned ship. Nothing like a magic user to get ya in trouble. That's the truth. I spend my time either cursin' him or my stomach."

"Speaking of stomachs," Parker interjected, "mine is screaming at me. All I've had to eat is Karl's cooking, and the rearick aren't necessarily known for their delicacies."

"Yah miss yer mum, lowlander," Karl said with a grin.

"Not as much as I miss yours."

Karl laughed low. "Dear girl's been dead fer years. And, scheisse, she would have torn ya to shreds, pretty boy."

"If she's anything like you... Anyway, I was thinking," Parker said, looking back over to Hannah, "maybe a group of us could head to the surface. See what we can find. I learned a thing or two about living off the land while we were back at the tower. I'll go, take Laurel with me. Bet she could hunt up some spices for us, make our little friend's cooking a bit more palatable."

Hannah eyed the ground beneath them and thought of Hassan and the marauders. "I'll think on it, but since we need to pass some time, Karl, what do you say to some training sessions. It'll get your mind off your stomach."

"Aye, not a bad idea, though watchin' ya damned fools wave swords around like toddlers always makes me sick."

The snap of Laurel's rope rang out across the open-aired deck, its metal tip dangerously close to Parker's skull. Sliding to his left, he batted the druid's weapon away with the end of his magitech spear.

"Damn, girl. We're just practicing," he grunted, righting himself.

With the twist of her arm, she drew back the blade, wrapping its tail effortlessly into long dangling loops by her side. "I know. Just imagine if I actually took you seriously." She winked and began walking to her left. "Where I'm from, warriors train without holding back. You get stabbed? Too bad. It means you're too slow. Suck it up, heal it up, do it over."

"In other words, you're all a bunch of psychos," he replied.

She laughed. "No. In other words, you'll never beat me."

As they circled, the two kept their eyes on one another, watching for an opportunity to strike. Parker stomped hard with his right foot, feigning attack, in an attempt to get her stuck on her back foot, but the girl didn't bite. When she joined the group, Laurel was already a better fighter than any of them, save for maybe Karl. On the battlefield, he was grateful for her, but currently, he wished someone else were toe-to-toe with her.

"Come on, ya bastard. If you can't take a tiny lass, I don't want ya in the shit with me," Karl shouted from the railing, a mug of ale in his meaty hand. Hannah was right, the training distracted him from his airsickness.

Without a look, Laurel extended her arm in the rearick's direction. With perfect aim and distance, the blade struck the mug just beneath his little finger. The sound of metal on metal chimed in their ears and Parker watched as the mug went sailing through the air.

"I'm not a damned lass, rearick," she said with a slight bow. "Next one will take off that little sausage pinkie of yours. Got it?"

Karl, inspired by Laurel's spunk and the mystic's brew, laughed deeply. "Scheisse! Ya got it, ma'am. And I'll take you into the heat of battle any day—maybe even into Ophelia's for a drink on a Friday night."

She glanced over at him and batted her eyes playfully. Parker took the chance to blast a beam of magitech power over her shoulder, forcing Laurel to dodge in haste. He followed his attack and landed a knee to her torso, pulling back at the last moment so as not to hurt her.

"Uh oh," Parker said playfully. "Looks like someone's a little slow."

Stumbling backwards, Laurel rolled onto her feet before he could get a jump on her. "You shouldn't pull your punches," she said as her rope-blade flashed through the air, wrapping Parker's legs at the ankle. With a sharp tug, she pulled his feet out from underneath him, sending Parker to the deck with a crash. Smiling, she said, "No lessons learned if my opponent hits like a bitch."

"Nice landing," Hadley said as he approached clapping. "You lowlanders know how to make an impact!"

Parker sat up with his hands raised and legs underneath him. "I give," he said to Laurel before turning back to the mystic. "Maybe it's time you step into the ring with her."

"I'm more of a lover than a fighter, and Sir Gregory seems to have staked his claim on this one." Hadley nodded to the slight druid.

She raised a middle finger and narrowed her eyes. "No one claims me, airhead. And, yes, you best keep out of the ring, I'd hate to mess your hair."

The men all laughed as she stepped back and leaned against the rail. Although she was the newest member of Hannah's group, Laurel took no time at all settling into her role and endearing herself to the rest of the members.

She was playful and kind, but had a tongue sharper than her blade. While she was away from the only home she'd ever known, Laurel felt at ease with the group. Although it was clear she missed having her hands in the dirt. Her words grew sharper with each day they remained airborne.

Just as Parker's heart was slowing from the fight, Sal flew in from the west, an animal twitching in his jaws. The dragon landed hard and dropped a giant deer with an enormous rack to the deck, and sat back, panting like a dog in heat.

Laurel rushed over and knelt by the animal, whose eyes darted about. "Thank you for your sacrifice," she whispered. "It won't be forgotten." Placing her hands on the buck's back, her eyes turned green, and the animal stopped moving.

Parker saw her eyes grow glassy and realized just how close the druids are to the animal world. As if he knew the situation, Sal lumbered over and pushed on her with his muzzle. Laurel smiled in response.

"These things are needed," she said with a sad smile. "You did your job, mighty dragon. Next time, end its life. Suffering is bad for all living things."

Sal nodded, sat, and drooped his head toward the deck. Parker could only assume the dragon understood the exchange precisely. Then, as if to break the tension, Laurel's cloak started to move. She laughed as Devin, her squirrel, poked its head out of the neckline of her cloak. Black, beady eyes darting about, she snuck back into the folds of Laurel's clothes. Moments later, she popped out of the sleeve and ran over to Sal, only to jump on the dragon's back and scurry up to his head.

They all laughed as they watched the dragon try to knock the animal off.

"That odd couple ought to get their own damn room," Karl grumbled from the railing.

Laurel scrunched her nose. "Well, that's a terrifying thought. Could you imagine what their kids would be like? Sal's strength with Devin's violence."

Parker laughed along with the rest, but then his eyes turned to Hannah.

I wonder what our kids would be like? Parker thought. A snicker from Hadley caught his attention, and he turned to see the mystic shaking his head.

Shut up, he thought as loudly as he could. The mystic started to laugh.

Dark circles sat heavy under Gregory's eyes as he held the stick steady. Being the only one who really knew how the *Unlawful* worked, or had been able to get a handle on the controls, certainly had its disadvantages.

Over the week and change they had been flying, he could count on his fingers and toes the number of hours he had slept, and although there were others who could learn to fly it, he had a particular leaning toward keeping his father's masterpiece in his own hands.

"What the hell does this do, dad?" Gregory mumbled as his fingertip played over a dial he had not yet dared to turn Everything else was accounted for, and they had even taken a few shots of the amphorald powered cannon at some deserted plains—just to test it. But the knob he caressed was unaccounted for, and frankly, Gregory feared turning it with his life.

"Still no idea, huh?"

Hearing Hannah's voice, he jumped in his chair, finger still shaking mid-air.

He breathed heavily. "Shit. I wish you wouldn't surprise me like that."

Hannah couldn't hold in a giggle. "Sorry. You know you look worse than my father did after an all-month bender, right?"

Gregory pushed his left hand awkwardly through his dark, kinky hair and tucked his trembling right between his legs. "Not a surprise, though I bet your pa had a few more shits and giggles than I have."

"Nah. He was an angry drunk... I've got some scars to prove it." She nodded back to the mystery device on the dash. "Get it over with. Turn the damned thing."

His mouth dropped open slightly. "Can't. No idea what it does."

"So? You didn't know what the other things were either when you started pulling, pushing, and turning. What makes this so different?"

He waved his left hand. "Come here." Hannah obliged and stood over him, looking at the controls. "The rest makes sense. Would have to my dad. Everything is precisely where it should be." Reaching between his legs he grabbed the stick that directed the ship up and down and laterally. He forced a grin. "Precisely where it should be. And this," he grabbed a lever with his right hand, "is the accelerator. Again, perfectly positioned. I can go through all of these devices and configure a reason for their positioning. It's damned brilliant, really."

"But that…" Hannah pointed.

Gregory scrunched his nose and continued to stare at the dial up and off to the left. "Makes no sense. And look—" he waved a finger over the control panel immediately in front of him "—there's still plenty of space."

Hannah reached out and grabbed the knob. "What the hell? If it blows…"

"No!" Gregory screamed, his eyes wide.

"Chill. I would never. It's just, either touch it or stop obsessing over it… actually, I could give you the same advice about Laurel." She tried a grin on, but he didn't respond. Placing her hand on his shoulder, she lowered her voice. "You're doing great. Don't worry. Zeke thinks we're making great time, and if the Oracle is really all-knowing, then I'm sure she'll tell you exactly what that thing does. Hell, it might open the glory hole."

"Glory what?"

"Must be a Boulevard thing. Ask Parker to show you," she said with a grin. "Listen, I came to see if everything else was OK with the ship."

Finally, Gregory smiled uncomfortably. "Yeah. Everything is good. Almost too good. My father thought of everything, like that's a surprise. He was the best freaking engineer Arcadia has ever seen."

"Second best."

"Thanks," Gregory's smile brightened.

"Oh, shit, no, I meant Maddie. I imagine she's home sharpening her skills as we speak."

He laughed fully. "I hate you."

"I love you, too." She gave him a little smack across the back of the head. "I'm glad the ship is in tip-top shape, but the crew is going nutso. Nobody's used to being cooped up like this, and I think there might be a mutiny just so people can put their feet down on solid ground for ten paces or so."

Gregory rubbed his hand against his teenage stubble. "Yeah... Laurel hasn't been sleeping well. I think it is because she's been detached from nature for so long. You know, it's wearing her down."

"And... you know this from firsthand experience?" Hannah said with a snicker.

He turned bright red and mumbled, "If only."

"Someday, Gregory. Takes patience to win a lady."

"What would you know about that?" Gregory laughed. "I think you're right, though. Time on the ground could do everyone some good. But, do you need to check with Ezekiel about it?"

Hannah slid into the co-pilot's seat and crossed her legs. "Of course. And you know what that means. Everything is on a tight schedule because of the Coming Darkness, whatever the hell that is. Probably no time to stop."

Looking down at the controls, Gregory said, "Slow is smooth, and smooth is fast," under his breath.

"What? Some kind of riddle?"

His head snapped up and turned in her direction. "Something my father always said when he was teaching me stuff. I always tried to get things done quickly. Messed them up more often than not. He'd always say that, over and over." Gregory made his voice an octave deeper. "'Slow is smooth, and smooth is fast, son. It's the secret to life.' Maybe he was right. If we just take a breath for a second, it would serve us well in the end."

"I thought his motto was sacrifice everything for the sake of the crazy Chancellor." Hannah grinned at her joke, but her friend cast his eyes at the floor. She cleared her throat. "Right. Sorry."

"No biggie. And, you're right. I won't be like him, you know. I can disconnect." But as he said this his eyes glanced at the knob up and to the left of where he was sitting.

Hannah stood and put her hand back on his shoulder. "I know. You're not him. We need you, and this— she waved around the cockpit "—is yours now."

"Thanks, Hannah."

"Don't mention it. Now I'm going to go meet with Zeke, right after I tell Laurel you've been watching her sleep."

He smiled sheepishly. "If I did watch her sleep, it would probably keep me awake. I almost fell asleep here a second ago."

"Why don't you just get her to make you some more of that kaffe?" Hannah asked. The druid's potent brew could do wonders.

"Are you kidding me? After what happened last time? Sal got one whiff and almost tore the ship apart."

"Yeah... that dragon sure does love his kaffe. I think we'd be safer taking our chance on the ground."

***

Reaching the aft cabin at the back of the boat, Hannah lifted her fist but paused before knocking.

"Come in," Ezekiel's voice rasped from behind the oak door.

Hannah touched the knob and could have sworn she felt the tingle of magic in the metal. She pushed the door open to find Ezekiel, sitting crossed legged on the bed, hands resting in his lap. His face was softer than she had remembered, kinder.

Directing the battle at the tower had taken a lot out of him, and the final assault on the Academy almost finished him. Now, sitting in the comfortable little cabin in the back of the boat, he looked more like the old man who had whisked her away from the Boulevard a year earlier.

It might have been her imagination, but his hair even seemed darker.

She looked around the room, seeing how he had settled in with everything in its right place and even some decorations. "Cozy little nook you've made yourself here, Zeke. Never knew you had a flare for design." She reached up and grabbed a porcelain owl from the top of a shelf. "Really?" she asked, raising a brow. "Cliche much?"

Ezekiel ignored her. "Grab a seat," he said, waving toward the empty chair across from the bed.

"I've kind of been wondering why you get your little room to yourself when the rest of us are piled on top of each other."

He nodded, and Hannah thought she saw the corners of his mouth turn up, if only slightly. "Well, if I were just sleeping and making dick jokes like the rest of you heathens, that would be fine. But most of my time in here is meditating. You may not know this about me, but I'm quite powerful. You don't want me losing focus."

"Hey, my dick jokes take a tremendous amount of concentration, too." Hannah huffed sarcastically and then joined him for a laugh. "Keeping connected with Lilith?"

"Trying. We're not close enough yet, at least I don't think so. But soon we will be. I need to keep trying, and I cannot be interrupted. This work is harder than anything you've experienced."

"Of course," she said with a wave of her hand. "I can keep those heathens away from you. But everybody is kind of going ape shit around here."

"Ape shit?"

"Yeah. You know, nucking futs." From the look on his face, she could tell he wasn't following. "Listen, we got on this boat over a week ago. All you told us is we're going to Lilith and something about something called the Darkness something. See how that might be disconcerting?"

He gave a slight nod. "And…"

"And… well, I think they just need something."

"And…"

"Damn it, Z. And… that's why I'm here."

The old man's brow furrowed, which turned to a smile. "Ah! You want me to do something about it."

"You know, Zeke, for the smartest damned person in Irth, you're pretty thick sometimes."

Ezekiel's smile grew. "Well, I'm sure you'd like it if I stepped in, now wouldn't you? But Hannah, I cannot always be the one giving direction. This is your team now, not mine. They need to follow you today, since I don't know where I might be tomorrow."

She leaned back in her chair and put her feet up on the bed. "OK. So, you're going to back whatever I tell them?"

"I trust you. Do what you know. What is your gut telling you?"

She uncrossed her feet and placed them on the floor. Leaning forward she said, "My gut's telling me I'm hungry. Time for a meeting."

CHAPTER THREE

Every seat in the makeshift mess hall was full for the first time since they had left Arcadia. Even Gregory, having slowed the ship and fastened the controls, showed up. They were all stuffing their faces, while Hannah looked on at her team.

Nothing about them looked special, especially when Karl spilled a line of soup down the front of his cloak, but they were hers... and they were among the most powerful people in all of Irth—as far as she had seen.

Once all were nearly done, she stood to speak. "I've come to a decision. It's time for a little field trip, everyone."

"A what?" Karl asked between bites of a hunk of venison bigger than Laurel's squirrel.

"Field trip. You know, get off the *Unlawful* for a bit. I expect most of you need to stretch your legs. And I realize if we stay here much longer, a lot of crazy shit is gonna go down. Not to mention, we could use any supplies you might be able to scavenge." She turned to Laurel. "And I was hoping you might be able to find some herbs to add some spice to Karl's grub."

She nodded. "Amazing how a spicy rearick is able to make the blandest food I've ever tasted."

"Tastes fine to me," he grumbled through a full mouth.

Her eyes cut to Ezekiel who was watching her work her team. It struck her that none of them were looking to him for guidance. "Good. Well then. First thing tomorrow, you'll all head down and see what you can come up with."

Clearing his throat, Gregory said, "If it's OK, I think I should stay here. Keep an eye on the ship."

She looked him over. Just being outside of the cockpit made her friend look a bit more like himself, but she was nevertheless concerned. "You sure? A break could do you some good. Smooth is slow and... Dammit. Something like that."

He grinned. "I'm fine. And if we're just going to hover, I can get out of the cockpit for a while. I want to run some diagnostics on the core anyway. It will be a good break to have."

"Right. Well, I'll stay, too, in case you need assistance."

"I'll stay, too," Parker blurted out. Everyone looked at him strangely. "You know, for assistance."

Karl snorted. "Right. I'm sure it's the *Unlawful* you're wanting to tinker with."

Everyone laughed, except for Hannah and Parker. Their cheeks went red, and they refused to make eye contact.

Hadley chimed in and broke the tension. "What about you, Ezekiel?"

The master magician pulled his pipe from his leather satchel and started to fill the bowl. He looked up at the mystic for a second before turning his attention back to his smoke. "I'm glad you asked." He lit the pipe and drew a long drag. Exhaling, he sent smoke and the fine scent of his herbs from the Heights dancing in the closed space. "I should apologize for being absent thus far on the trip. I have had much to attend to."

"Like what?" Hadley prodded.

A smile spread on Ezekiel's face. The mystic knew more than the others, he assumed. "Like trying to get in touch with the Oracle."

Karl nearly rolled his eyes out of his head. "Aye, wizard, about this Darkness you spoke of…"

Ezekiel held up a hand. "All in good time, friend. All in good time."

"Scheisse, I was afraid ya'd say that. Alright then. I'm off to try to get some sleep on this damned rocking heap." He glanced at Laurel and then to Hadley. "Looks like it's the three of us. We leave at sunrise."

Laurel smiled and quickly stood to follow, but Hadley stayed behind as the rest were heading out of the room.

I need to talk with you, he said in Hannah's mind.

She gave him a nod and said goodbye to the others as they left, until finally, only she and Hadley remained.

"What is it?" she asked with some concern.

Hadley shook his head. "Nothing too big, it's just…"

"Spit it out, weirdo."

He turned back toward the door to make sure no one was lingering outside. Hadley, normally laid back and fun-loving, looked unusually grave. "Keep your eye on Ezekiel."

She laughed. "No worries there. I'm always keeping one eye on the wiley old bastard. You just never know when he's going to…"

"No," Hadley interrupted. "I'm serious. What he's doing— trying to contact Lilith as he is—well, it's deadly."

"Deadly? Come on, stop being so melodramatic. You sound like a bunch of noble girls in the Academy."

"You don't get it. Think of your own powers, your physical magic. When you do something, something big, you feel it. Like when you finished off Adrien, drawing on as much power as you could."

"Yeah," she said. "I was exhausted for days after finishing off that asshat. But I recovered." She spread her hands out. "Here I am."

"Bodies recover pretty quickly from using the magic inside, at least relatively. The mind is different. The more you work your body, the longer you have to rest, but as far as we know it will always recover, but there are stories about old mystics who…"

"What?"

Hadley rubbed his hand across his chest as though he could feel his words at the core of his being. "There have been mystics who have pushed their mental magic to the limit—and beyond. Some of them recover, but it still leaves traces, residue of the energy they've used. But there are others who have just gone raving mad."

Hannah's eyes narrowed. "Not Ezekiel…"

"Maybe. He's strong, but also desperate. We don't know what is going on, but if he is in such a hurry to contact the Oracle, it seems he might push himself too far. We're weeks away from her. I know they have a special kind of connection, but that sort of reach could change his mind forever." He paused, letting his words hang for a moment. "I'm not trying to freak you out. All I'm saying is to keep an eye on him. Check in. And make sure he takes breaks between sessions, and no matter what, while he is focused, don't disturb him..."

Hannah nodded. "Got it. Don't want the old man to go all remnant on us."

He tilted his head. "Yeah, remnant would be nothing compared to some of the tales of a few mystics we lost before my time. Anyway, I need to get ready for the trip. Just be watchful."

After giving her arm a squeeze, Hadley left the room, leaving Hannah to wonder just how far the wizard would go to save Irth —and how far she would go.

A cool morning breeze blew across the deck as Parker watched the landing party get ready. Gregory landed the *Unlawful* in a clearing atop a small field, then joined them on the deck

Karl had already grabbed hold of the rope and was whistling as he climbed down to the ground below. Laurel was supposed to follow after, but she was lingering near Gregory.

Parker watched as the engineer awkwardly said goodbye to her.

"You sure you don't want to come?" she asked, grabbing his hand. "Could be nice... walking through the woods together. I could use your help. What if I get lost?"

"Um, yeah. No. No. It's better if I stay with the ship. Plus, I'm sure someone with your tracking skills will be just fine. Just keep an eye on where the sun is."

Rolling her eyes, she dropped his hand and turned to leave. "Great advice."

Just as she was about to jump over the side, Gregory blurted out. "Wait."

"Yeah?" she asked hopefully.

"While you're out there, um, you should look for some medicinal plants, too. Can never be too cautious."

She sighed. "Yes, you can." Then with a swift jump, she slid down the rope.

Hadley was last to go. "I respect your decision to stay aboard the ship, Hannah. But don't worry. I'll give you the play by play." He turned to look at Parker, but was still addressing her. "I'll do my best to stay in your head the whole time."

"That's sweet, Had," she said.

Parker rushed over, nearly pushing him down the rope. "OK, OK, time to go. Daylight's a wasting. Safe trip and everything. Don't fall and hit your head on the way down!"

When they were alone, Hannah turned and looked at him funny. "What the hell was that all about? And why aren't you going? You've been dying to get off this ship."

Parker smiled sheepishly. "What? Can't a guy help out his friend? I was just wishing him the best of luck. And besides, I've seen plenty of the world. Too much, maybe. I'd much rather stay here. You know, spend some time meditating or something."

Hannah sighed and shook her head. "Meditating? You may have been the best con artist the Boulevard has ever seen, but you're shockingly bad at lying. You know that?"

"Aye, feels damned good to have me feet on solid ground," Karl said as he watched Parker and Hannah pull the ropes back up into the ship. The ship began to hum, then took off a minute later.

Karl stretched his arms back and drew in a deep breath of foreign air.

"Tell me about it," Laurel quipped as she slipped off her shoes and felt the connection with the natural surroundings.

She knelt to the ground and ran her fingers through the long grass of the field they had just lowered into. Karl could hear her mumble something, and Devin, her squirrel, crawled out of her leather bag and rolled around in the grass.

The rearick shook his head, still unsure of what he thought of the druids. He thought the mystics were strange, holed up in the temple, gazing at their navels. But compared to the young woman talking to the grass and laughing with her pet, those mindnuts seemed perfectly sane. "Don't get *too* comfortable there, princess wilderness. We got some work to do, after all!"

Laurel, smiling like a child, ignored him as she rolled over and closed her eyes in the tall grass. He snorted in response and turned to take in their surroundings.

Gregory had done well to land them in a field at the top of a small rise. Spring had come to the region, sooner than it would have made it to the Arcadian valley, and Karl knew just how far away from the Heights he was. The hills rolled off in either direction, a stand of pines growing up around them. Further off to the north, a crag of rocks grew up out of the boughs, the dark rocks warmed by the morning sun.

Laurel tugged on his sleeve and broke him from his admiration of the rocks which looked nothing like the stones he knew so well in the Heights.

"Looks like we both want to go that way." She smiled. "I'd like to get into those trees, and you're looking at that rock face like a man looks at a beautiful woman."

"Aye, child. Rocks are often better company. Steady, reasonable, and they don't say much."

She smacked him on the arm playfully, but with enough force to cause a sting through his leather cloak. "No wonder you're still alone, Karl. It's your preference for hardened rock over anything soft and tender."

"Nah," Hadley finally chimed in. "I've seen the women of Craigston enough to know that that outcropping is frail in comparison to any of the women Karl's been with."

The rearick laughed and patted his hammer. "This girl right here is the only company I need."

"Well, someday, I'll introduce you to a woman from the Forest who will blow your mind... among other things." She raised her brow. "We have a way about us."

"Scheisse, lass. With a mouth like that..."

She held up her hand. "Stop right there. I don't want to hear Hadley's jokes on this one. Now, before we spend any more time on Karl's love life, let's get moving. We don't have much time before we need to be back here for the pickup. Beyond those trees, down the rise, sits the sea. I say we take to the pines, see what we can find there, and then skirt close to the rocks toward the water."

"How the hell do you know all of that?" Hadley asked.

"Ah, mystic, you're connected to the minds of others, my connection is with nature herself. Did you think I was just taking a nap there in the grass? It's what we call communion, and the flora has more stories to tell than you can imagine."

Karl shook his head and snorted, unsure whether or not to believe her story. "Aye, let's get ta work then. If we were underground, I'm sure I'd be takin' the lead. But the forests belong to you. Take the lead, lass."

Laurel nodded her approval, and without a command, Devin took off toward the line of trees with her master on her heels. Karl and Hadley followed in silence and watched the druid as she wove her way between the thick pines that made up the canopy overhead. Little grew beneath their boughs, but the druid would crouch in a little patch of undergrowth, plucking handfuls of herbs good for cooking.

"She ain't bad, really," Karl finally said, growing tired of the silence.

Hadley nodded. "Yep. I wouldn't want to be on the other side of her wrath, that's for sure. And if she can find a thing or two to add flavoring to your bland meat, well, I'm not gonna throw her overboard."

"My meat is just fine," Karl grunted. "Thank ya very much! And 'tis an important role, cookin' and all. I just can't help but wonder what good ya are to the group, mind jockey. I got me hammer and the girl a whip. I still haven't seen you do much of nothin' in a fight."

Hadley laughed. "Short and short-sighted, are you, Karl? I think you've seen the mystics contribute often enough in and out of battle with our gifts."

"Blood on the ground. That's the only contribution that really matters when a fight breaks out. And if we run into an angry bear or something out here, then what? The girl would likely tame it with her nature magic, my hammer is magic enough. What are you going to do? Read its mind or something? Try to talk it down?"

Hadley continued walking, lengthening his stride to mess

with the short-legged rearick. "Nah, you'd stand a better chance at that, Karl."

"Oh?"

"Well, it seems the mind of a bear is closer to a rearick than a typical human," Hadley said with a grin. "And they look alike, too."

Karl failed at his attempt not to smile. "Yer a sonofabitch."

"Yeah, you're probably right... But she was my mum, so watch your mouth. Otherwise I'll twist your brain and make it so you only eat vegetables." Hadley slowed and glanced over his shoulder. Karl looked outright nervous at that suggestions, so Hadley flashed his eyes white. "Besides, my role here isn't to kill bears. My job is to let Hannah know where we are. If we get into a world of shit, you'll be glad when I can call in the cavalry."

Karl watched his friend's face lose all affect, and he knew that Hadley was connecting with Hannah back on the ship. "I'm telling ya, kid..." Karl began to say to the mystic in his trance, but before he could finish the sentence, a rock the size of Karl's fist flew in from nowhere, knocking Hadley to the dirt.

"Shit!" the rearick screamed as he pulled his hammer from his hip and turned placing his body in between the bleeding mystic and whatever hell was waiting for them.

Hannah held a finger up at Sal. "Wait."

His tail swept to the side across the deck of the ship. his eyes fastened on the bucket in her arms.

"Stand clear of that weapon," Gregory said, watching the spiked tail. "He's dangerous even when he doesn't know it."

"He's a freaking kitty cat," Hannah said, her finger still raised. She looked down at Sal. "Sit." She said. He responded immediately. "Good boy."

"What's next?" Parker asked from his seat on the railing. "You gonna start playing fetch?"

"Hey, you guys train up here all the time. No reason I can't try to teach this old dog new tricks." She glanced back at the dragon. "Sit up."

Sal shook his head and stayed seated.

"OK, pal, no sitting up, none of this." She nodded at the bucket.

Sal paused and glanced over at the guys.

Parker shrugged. "Don't look at us, Sal. She's your human. I've been trying to train her since we were three. It's useless."

Dipping his head, Sal gave her one last glance. Knowing cute would never win the day, Sal sat up on his haunches, front legs hanging in front of him awkwardly. Hannah responded with a deep laugh, followed by her spilling the leftovers of the deer Sal himself had hunted for them on the deck. The dragon kept his eyes on her.

"OK. Now! Get it."

He dove at the pile of remains and starting chomping on the pile, bones, skin, and all.

"You're cruel," Gregory said as she walked over to them. "It won't be long before he realizes that he can just eat the deer he catches—worse he'll understand he can make all of us sit up and roll over for the food he brings us."

Hannah smiled. "When that day comes, I'll be happy to play pup for him. Until then, I'll keep reminding him who holds the leash."

"Speaking of being kept on a leash, what the hell is going on with you and Laurel?" Parker asked Gregory. "I mean, is that actually happening?"

The young engineer turned bright red as he turned to look out over the horizon. "I kind of have my hands full with the ship right now. Not to mention, I…"

"What?" Hannah asked, bumping her hip across his. "Oh, wait. Hell, are you not into—"

"I AM!" Gregory yelled. "I mean... women. Yes. I am." Gregory stuttered like the early days of their friendship.

"Ladies and gentlemen, old Gregory has returned." She tousled his hair into a mess. "Don't worry about it. Parker here has never known how to talk to women."

Parker snorted. "Guess that's why I've spent most of my life talking to you, Hannah." He turned back to Gregory. "Listen, I don't want to push you, but it seems like Laurel really likes you. I mean she laughs at your jokes, which aren't really that funny, and she always seems to be checking in on the cockpit."

"You said 'cockpit'," Hannah snorted.

Parker glared at her. "Do you mind? I'm trying to educate my man here." Turning back to Gregory, he said, "Maybe you should just let her know how you feel."

"Yeah," Hannah said. "I mean all the dudes on this ship are totally excellent at telling women how they feel."

Gregory ignored her and looked up at Parker. "I've just, well, never done this before." He finally turned to Hannah. "Remember when you were trying to learn how to dance?"

"I'm trying to forget... So, thanks."

"That's what this feels like. I keep thinking I need to do something, but I've never done it before. Just like dancing, I think I know how to do it, but it's still so damned foreign."

Parker put his hand on Gregory's shoulder. "Don't worry, man. It will come."

Hannah snickered. "It will come. *Zing!*"

"By the Matriarch!" Parker shouted. "Are you a thirteen-year-old boy, or what?"

"Or what," Hannah replied with a grin.

Gregory laughed and Parker shot her a glare. She knew he was speaking not only to Gregory, but probably to her as well— and himself. The romantic tension had ebbed and flowed between them since puberty, but there was nothing like the shared fight for the universe to bring two people together.

Her eyes cut back over to Parker and his glare had turned to something different. Something like longing. But what did she know about such things?

And as usual, as of late, her thoughts of Parker were interrupted by Hadley.

Hey, captain. How are things topside?

Hannah closed her eyes and thought her response. *Tip top. How's your field trip?*

No problems down here. The druid seems to have new life breathed into her. The only thing is... Suddenly, Hadley's communication trailed off.

Hadley? She called back. *Hadley? What's the thing?*

He came back. *Cool your jets, beautiful. Except... I might just punch your rearick friend in his little, yellow teeth before all is done down here.*

She laughed, and her mind quickly wandered from Parker to the mystic—once mysterious and attractive, now, just damned attractive.

Take it easy on him, OK. Same time for pick up?

Yeah. Laurel is working the ground, pulling weeds like...

And then there was nothing.

Hadley? Stop dicking around. What's going on?

She waited, glancing to Parker, then to Gregory, and then toward the ground beneath them.

"What did he say?" Parker asked. He had become accustomed to the look on her face when the mystic was speaking in her head, and, when he was honest with himself, he didn't really like it.

"Don't know. He just—" Hannah grabbed her head in her hands and screamed. She fell to her knees.

Gregory and Parker rushed to her side, and Sal looked up from the spot on the deck where she had dumped the food.

"What is it?" Parker asked, pulling her into an embrace.

"He's gone," she whispered.

"Gone?"

"Don't know. Got cut short. Something's happened to them." Hannah sat up and grabbed Parker's hand. "We need to go after them."

Before he could answer, Gregory jumped in. "Laurel," he grunted. "We have to go."

Hannah shifted her eyes to him. "Gregory, no. You need to get us down there, and then get the ship out of range. We have no idea what's waiting for us, and the ship is too valuable to risk."

"But—"

"Have you seen me in action?" she said with a smile. "I'll bring your hot, little, wood nymph back. But we need this ship in one piece."

Gregory furrowed his brow in concentration and nodded. "But don't come back without her."

"If she's not with me, I won't come back." Hannah patted him on the shoulder. She stood and starting walking to get her things. Stopping, she turned to him. "And Gregory, no matter what, do not wake Zeke up."

Hannah saw his face go pale, but then Gregory gritted his teeth. "I've got this."

CHAPTER FOUR

Parker worked his way down the rope, hand-over-hand, as his muscles burned. The ship had a large door that opened at ground level, but it was a pain to get open. A large crank had to be turned by hand, and it took damned near forever. So, most of the time, they opted for climbing the rope.

Looking down, between his legs, he saw Hannah sitting, legs crossed, leaning against her dragon. She had said that Sal couldn't handle both of them, but he had a sneaking suspicion that she just wanted to see him struggle his way down the line.

When his boots finally hit the ground, he heard her clapping. "Nice finish!" She laughed as Sal snorted in his direction.

He bowed and then walked toward her. "Why don't you two get off your asses so we can go find our friends?"

"Just waiting for you."

They waved as Gregory lifted the ship in the air. Parker knew Hannah wasn't in love with the idea of Gregory guarding their most precious asset all by himself. But Parker figured that as long as he stayed above the clouds, there was very little that could go wrong.

They left the grassy spot on the top of the rise where they had last seen Karl, Laurel, and Hadley only hours ago. Hannah cut off for the north. It was all she knew, except for the fact that she had received the message from Hadley not too long after they had dropped them for their simple mission. They couldn't have gotten far.

She reached out with her mind for the mystic but got nothing. Her heart was as heavy as her footfalls as they walked toward the pine forest.

"We'll find them," Parker said, assuring himself as much as he was her.

"I know. And, if something happened to them, there'll be hell to pay."

The shade of the pines greeted them, and Hannah was glad for it. While it was still only early spring, the air was hotter and heavier than in the Arcadian Valley. She and Parker walked silently through the needle-covered floor, both of them searching for some clues of where their friends may have gone, and what might have caused the disconnection of her and Hadley.

"There," Parker said. His keen eye picking out a place where a patch of undergrowth had been picked. "Laurel's been here."

Hannah only nodded and pushed on, looking for more places that the druid might have harvested the weeds that might someday season their food. They followed the trail that she had inadvertently left behind. Sal bounded beside them, sniffing in the dirt. They crept from one patch to another until it led them to a spot in the forest where the trees met the outcropping of rocks to their right.

"Trail ends here," Parker said.

A branch snapped somewhere in the distance, and Sal took off running. Parker opened his mouth to yell for him, but Hannah just laughed it off. "He's probably just hunting for rabbit or something. He'll be fine. And this way, he won't step all over the evidence."

Hannah searched the ground where they were standing. The

needles, which mostly lay spread out over the forest floor as if carefully strewn, were a mess where they stood. Marks were made as if a great dance had taken place upon them.

"There was a fight here."

Parker nodded. "You're right. This is where it happened. Where Hadley was cut off."

"We're close then."

Parker's eyes scanned the rock wall overhead. The sun danced off its surface and created dark lines, indicating deep seams in the otherwise smooth surface. He wondered if the rearick had somehow scaled the surface and crawled into a cave to have a little piece of home surrounding him. The thoughts of Karl left, as a scream filled the air.

"Trespassers," the high, shrill voice cried, just as a rock shot from one of the seams toward them.

Whoever had thrown it had the aim of a master marksman. Parker would have taken it in the face, if not for Hannah's quick thinking. A shield of glowing blue rose up around them, deflecting the rock off onto the forest floor—and then another and another.

"The hell?" he shouted.

"Quite the welcome," Hannah said, scanning the rocks for their attackers.

She didn't have to look long. A body emerged from a crease thirty feet over their heads. Whoever, or whatever was attacking them, quickly scrambled down the rock face. Its proportions, even as it moved quickly, looked anything but ordinary. There was a torso the size of a normal person, but their arms and legs were long, as if they had been stretched out on a torture device.

Landing on the ground, the figure crouched, staring at them. Although its body looked completely abnormal, its face was clearly that of a young girl. There was a wild look in her eyes, a look that Parker recognized. It was the same look he saw in Hannah's as she lay in the streets of Arcadia after the murder of her brother. This kid—or creature—wanted revenge or restitution.

And if the look in her eye didn't prove it, the fact that she charged them was a clear sign.

Hannah kept her shield up, but the girl didn't know it was there. As she dove to attack them, Hannah shifted the barrier, sending their attacker's body, with its gangly limbs, sprawling on the pine needle floor.

The girl sprang to her feet, another rock already in her left hand. It was then that Parker noticed her right hand was missing —half the arm in fact, cut off just after the elbow.

What the hell? he thought.

Dropping the shield, Hannah raised her hands. "Wait! We only want to talk. We've lost our friends."

"Yeah, well, join the club. I've lost something, too. And I want him back."

Hannah glanced at Parker who shrugged. Before they had a second to discuss the situation, the girl pulled a knife from her belt and threw it. Her aim with the rocks paled in comparison to her precision with a blade.

Parker ducked, barely dodging the attack. "Shit, kid. Knock it off. You don't know what you're up against."

"Don't matter," the kid snarled. "We want him back." With that, she rushed them again, bloodlust in her eyes.

Wisely, the kid chose Parker as his target.

Parker spread his legs wide in a defensive pose and waited for the attack.

Springing, the kid launched herself at Parker, whose arms were outstretched. Just as she neared the Arcadian, Parker grabbed the folds of her cloak and rolled, throwing his attacker behind him into the trunk of a pine. As the kid struggled to get up, Parker pulled his magitech spear from his back and leveled it at her. At the same time, Hannah pulled her arms across her chest, shaping two fireballs, one in each hand.

41

"Don't," Hannah said. "You better stop before you get seriously hurt."

The girl's eyes cut from Hannah to Parker and back. "You won't get away with it," she said just before turning and springing into the pines.

Parker took aim on her with his weapon, but Hannah pushed its barrel toward the ground. "No. We need her."

Looking up at his friend, Parker realized what she was thinking. Without a word, they dusted themselves off, and proceeded to follow the girl into the woods.

Sal crashed through a second later, a large, dead bird hanging from his teeth.

"Real nice," Parker said. "You're supposed to be our watchdog, and instead you're out gorging yourself on wild game."

Sal looked at him, then swallowed the bird in one bite—feathers and all.

"See," Hannah said. "You were mean to him, so you don't get to share in his hunt."

Parker thought for a second about swallowing a bird's beak whole. "Poor me."

Karl leaned his head against solid wooden bars which divided him from freedom, and, for the first time in over a week, he wished he was aboard the airship. At least there he could drink himself to sleep in his room when the druid was driving him crazy. Here, he was stuck with her.

Laurel paced back and forth in her own cell, only five feet away. She looked like a caged animal, wildly waiting for release back into its habitat. On the other side of him was another friend —Hadley. Only this one was slumped in the corner of the cell, still unconscious from the rock he took to the side of the head.

The bleeding had stopped, but the boy hadn't so much as stirred since the attack.

"Scheisse, lass. Stop with yer pacing already," he called out to Laurel. "It's driving me mad, and it ain't doing a shite of good."

She paused and looked up at him. For the first time since Laurel had joined them from the Dark Forest, her face seemed different. Drawn. Concerned. Karl had spent a day or two in lockup, but it was clear that the situation they were now in was something new for the girl, and Karl felt at least mildly responsible. He glanced beyond his bars and saw his hammer sitting in an open room, resting against the wall, begging for his companionship.

Although he blamed himself for their capture, deep down, he knew there was nothing he could have done. The first rock came out of nowhere, and the aim was perfect. It found its target on Hadley's temple, as if it were made for it, and dropped the mystic without warning. The rearick's hammer was out and at the ready before Hadley's body hit the ground, but it was no use.

Two dozen men, with stork like legs and arms hanging longer than Karl was high, stepped out of the shadows of the rocks. Years of battle had taught the rearick when to fight and when to put up his hands. The former occurred more often than the latter, but today was a day for surrender. Laurel felt differently.

She had already sprang into action. Her wicked rope work had sent one of them tumbling, and another was fighting off a small shrub. Luckily, Karl had gotten her to stop before someone was seriously hurt. Odds are this lot would have repaid blood for blood, and he felt responsible for his young companions.

Even though he knew his decision was the right one, he still cursed himself.

They bound he and Laurel with lashes of leather. Their work was silent, even though the feisty young druid demanded their response. From the first moment he saw them, Karl knew these were men on a mission, and that it wasn't their job to discuss terms with their captors. Even then, he second guessed himself. If he had engaged, the girl would have fallen suit. They'd have taken out a swath of the men, and, if all things worked to their advantage, they may have won. But chance is a bitch and luck a whore. Karl knew not to trust either.

Now, alone in his cell, he needed to figure out their next move. He paced his cage, taking note of every one of the bars, looking for a sign of weakness. There was always a point of frailty—in men, systems, and even in the prisons they shape. But the place in which he was held seemed to defy this law of the universe. Each bar was perfect, designed to thwart a mind such as his.

He hissed at Laurel. "Aye, what can ya do?" he asked.

She looked up at him and furrowed her brow.

He nodded, thankful for her attention. "With yer magic. These bars are wooden. Wood comes from nature. Bet ya can do somethin', right? Talk to 'em or turn 'em into flowers?"

The girl stared vacantly at him, lost in thought. She stopped pacing and focused on an invisible mark on the floor. After what felt like an eternity, she turned her eyes up to meet his. "Nobody should be held like this. No one."

"No shite. Maybe someday you can take it up with the Queen Bitch, but for now, she ain't here. But we are. And you need to focus your energy on getting us the hell outta here." He placed his finger on the bar that showed the most wear. "Right here. This is the weakest link. Can you make it a little less strong?"

Laurel narrowed her eyes inspecting the seams where the bars met the floor and ceiling. "Nature magic is all about life—that wood has been dead for years."

"Yeah, but Hannah could turn it into glass or something."

A playful smile spread across the druid's face. "Well, next time you decide to get captured, do it with Hannah."

"I just meant—"

"I know what you meant," she said. "But it just doesn't work like that, not for me. Maybe if we were at ground level—I could try and pull on some nearby roots to help us. But indoors, and at this height, I'm about as useless as you are."

"Good to know," Karl said. "Remind me why we brought you on this little quest?"

She smiled. "Because you love me." She looked at the bars again. "What the hell? I can give it a shot, I guess. Not much else going on here. And if it'll get you to stop sulking, it'll be worth it."

Karl watched as Laurel grabbed the bars of her own cell and focused her attention on his. Her eyes turned green as she attempted to connect with the natural elements in the bars holding them prisoner.

He muttered a prayer to whatever being might be listening under his breath and realized that his years of suspicion of magic had all been a waste of energy. It had saved his ass more than once before, and he hoped it might just work this time.

The bars in front of him began to grow warm, and he couldn't tell if his eyes were playing tricks on him, but they seemed to glow a little. He wasn't exactly sure what sort of connection she had with them, but there was something. Finally, Laurel exhaled in exhaustion and leaned against the wall of her cell.

"Sorry, no can do. Looks like we're stuck here."

"Well, thanks for trying," Karl said. "But let's not lose hope that easily. I might just have some magic up my sleeve, too."

He paced to the other side of his cell and grabbed a simple chair—the only furniture in this place—left by some sort of mercy by the guards. Wedging the front legs between the bars, Karl pushed, veins popping from his temples. He put all of his weight and muscle into the lever. And just as he was about to give in, he felt something give and then heard a loud *pop*.

It wasn't the bars, but the chair that gave up on the battle of wood on wood. As the the legs snapped off, Karl followed his weight and slammed against the bars. Nose throbbing, he shouted, "Blasted son of a scheisse!"

Laurel laughed. "That is one *impressive* magic trick. I'll have to remember it."

"Har har," he said as he sat on the ground and checked to see if his nose was broken. "Well, it looks like we've only got one thing left to do... we wait. Who knows what these long-legged bastards want with us, but we need to stay on alert. We bide our time, and keep a watchful eye out for our opportunity. I ain't dyin' here— and I ain't lettin' you or Hadley either. We're gonna bust our arses outta this damned place."

Laurel shrugged. "Or we wait for Hannah and Parker to do it for us."

Karl smiled. "Now, where's the fun in that?"

CHAPTER FIVE

Barely keeping the kid in sight, Parker followed her footsteps down the hill and toward the water that lay below. Hannah was just behind him, walking gently enough to be almost silent. Or maybe the lumbering of the dragon made enough noise to cover any sound either of them were making.

"Sal," he whispered. "Can you please be a little less noisy?"

The dragon stopped, looked at his taloned feet and then back up at Parker. He tilted his head and blinked twice.

"I didn't think so."

"Just keep moving," Hannah said. "The kid can't hear us from this far back. We'll be fine."

Parker scanned the trees, which were thinning out as they reached a clearing. The rock wall still stood, towering over them, and, as far as Parker could see, led straight down to the shoreline.

"I'm not worried about that one," Parker said, pointing ahead at the figure that cut through the rocks just down the hill. "If she were out here, who knows how many of them might be hiding in those rocks, even now?"

Hannah nodded and remained silent, which meant she had no answer for her old friend. He couldn't help but give her a grin, knowing that for once, he was right. They pushed on out of the cover of the pines and into a clearing that spread out before a steep drop.

They huddled behind a pile of rocks, looking down toward the ocean. The kid looked back twice, trying to see if she was followed as she trotted toward a small village rising out of the perfectly cobalt sea. Parker had never seen such a place before. To him, it was like something from the stories told when he was a child... A place where the ocean stretched off into forever and swallowed the horizon.

"Beautiful," he whispered.

Hannah crouched next to him. "Thanks, but I could use a bath right about now."

It was his turn to ignore her as he examined the village as carefully as he could from that distance. There were dozens of short houses. From their vantage point, they looked like something that he, Hannah, and Will would have made from sticks and grass in their childhood. A larger building, one built from stone, rose from the center. It looked austere in comparison to the low huts.

"That's where they'll be," he said, pointing at the building in the center of the city.

Hannah's eyes flashed red, and Parker knew exactly what she was doing. The psychic connection between her and Hadley was helpful, but he couldn't help but resent the special bond it created between them. They were in near constant communication, always sharing secret jokes with one another. While he had seen nothing to make him suspect their relationship was anything more than friends, just the glimmers of something in his imagination drove him mad.

"Nothing," she finally said, her eyes turning back to their normal color.

"Hell, maybe he isn't there. We never really considered that."

Hannah shook her head. "No. He's there. I couldn't reach him, but I just know it."

"Couldn't you do your mind-walking thing? Scope out the village that way?"

"Maybe," she said. "Although projecting myself that far is probably a bit beyond me. Not to mention the fact that I'd move almost as slow as if I were on foot."

Parker nodded. "Well, if magic can't do it, we'll try the old-fashioned way. You and the lizard stay here. I'll head into the town and see what I can find."

A scowl rose on her face. "No way you're going without us."

Parker looked at Sal. The dragon had his head low, like he was trying to hide, but his green, scaly ass was pointing straight into the air, clearly standing out overtop the sandy rocks. If the situation wasn't so dire, Parker would have hit the ground laughing.

"I don't think your pet is really built for stealth. He'd bring the village down on us in minutes. You two stay here. I'll head in and poke around. Keep your eye on the skies. If I need you, I'll give three quick blasts with my spear. At that point, I think Sal will be more than helpful."

Hannah bit her lip and considered the request for a moment. "OK," she finally said. "But don't hesitate. We've already lost half of our team. I don't want to lose you, too."

"Can't imagine life without me, huh?"

"What can I say? We need the numbers… Now, get your ass moving before I change my mind."

Parker reached down to grab her hand. Their fingers instinctively interlaced before he pulled away, turned, and jogged down the hill.

He thought back to the ass kicking Laurel had given him on the ship. He was getting better at fighting, and Gregory's tech helped a ton. But he would never be an all-star on the battlefield, not like Karl or the druid. But this… this was his element. Stealth and strategy—seeking out others' weaknesses and exploiting them.

That's what his friends needed right now, and that's what he had to offer.

As he neared the edge of the village, he ducked behind an empty hut that was positioned a little higher up the hill. It gave him a solid vantage point of the south side of town and a street that led to the building at the hub of the community. From where he knelt, he watched members of the village going about their day-to-day affairs.

They wore simple clothes, and each of them were built like the kid they met on the hill above him—thin, with strangely long legs and arms hanging down to their knees. But they also had huge hands and feet, giving them a frog-like appearance.

Parker had seen enough of the world to know people looked pretty different than they did in Arcadia. The rearick were all stocky and hairy—although they had the strength of a bull. Laurel was the only druid he knew, but he gathered enough from her stories to suspect that most of her people looked like her too —green eyes, fair skin, and just a hint of a point to their ears.

And here, in this tiny village, were the toad people.

He pictured the girl they followed and the way she was able to fly down the cliff face. Even with her amputated arm, her long reach—not to mention the strength in her good hand—must make climbing a breeze.

He imagined they'd be pretty badass swimmers as well.

Turning, he found a narrow passage between two rows of houses. It was something they would consider an alley in Arcadia, but the word didn't quite fit the tidy little village. He kept his head low, slinking slowly under open windows. With his short arms and legs and strange clothes, he knew it would be nearly impossible to simply meld in with the rest of the people. He was a foreigner from head to toe.

He kept to the shadows, something the setting sun made easy, and worked closer and closer to the center. As he crept to the edge of a major street, he could see the main building. A quick sprint and he would be there, but the sound of voices caught his attention. He dove for cover behind a large barrel.

"We gotta be careful," one voice, low and gravelly said. "Apparently, there are more around than those foreigners we caught on the hill. Heard Aysa shouting about it."

"Ah, she's crazy," another voice replied. "I wouldn't trust a word she said."

"Well, I don't know about you, but I'm not letting my kids wander the edges, especially after what happened to Samet."

Another voice, a bit higher, but just as rough, said, "Been years since we've seen outsiders, but Samet ain't exactly like you and me. I'm sure your little grubs are safe out there. Especially since the chief has got all of us on high alert."

The other man laughed. "Probably right, but I'm not taking chances. Who knows what these barbarians are after?"

The men kept talking, but Parker lost their conversation as they moved down the street. Seemed his friends—the barbarians—were certainly here. He turned his attention to the large building ahead of him. Peeking out from around the corner of the alley, he found the streets empty. He exhaled, jumped to his feet, and started at a sprint for the door at the front of the structure.

Relief set in as the knob turned. He dove inside, closed the door behind him, and dropped to the ground, listening for any sign of life inside the building.

Nothing. It was quiet.

He moved around on tiptoes. The first floor was empty, so he took a narrow staircase up. The wooden steps squeaked beneath him, and he held his breath as the climb terminated at a closed door at the top. He pulled his magitech staff from his back, turned the knob, and stepped through into blinding light.

The door opened to a narrow hall that was covered on one

side by windows. Just ahead, he could see it opened into a bigger room. What lay beyond that was what interested him. Through an open door, he could see the outline of what looked like bars— as good of an indication as any that he had found his friends.

He stepped into the room, but his eyes caught movement to the right. Parker tried to raise his staff in defense, but he was slow compared to the long, swinging arm of the guard who was waiting for him.

One hand lashed out—bigger than Karl's head—and swiped the spear from Parker's hand. The other landed a fist as hard as rock on his temple. The world spun, and Parker dropped.

———

Karl's head jerked toward the hall when he heard a crash followed by the sound of a fist on flesh. "Damn it," he shouted at Laurel. "I believe that's our cue."

Jumping from the single cot in her cell, she walked over to the bars, straining to see down the hall. "Sounds like something's going down out there."

"Aye, and we're here pickin' our asses."

She gave him a strange look. "Well, you can keep picking your ass. But I'm getting us out of here." She pulled on the folds of her cloak. "All right, girl. It's time."

Devin poked her head out from the neckline, and she scrambled out onto the druid's shoulder. Tilting her head, Laurel whispered something to the squirrel, and she responded by scrambling down to the floor. In a flash, she slipped through the bars and was gone from the room.

"Should only take a second," Laurel said to the confused rearick.

"I ain't even gonna ask. But it better work. Now that you've had a moment to rest, anything you can do for him?" Karl nodded toward Hadley, who was still unconscious in his own cell.

She exhaled long and hard. "Healing isn't really my strong suit. Certainly not from this distance." She grinned as Devin returned with a glimmer of metal in her mouth. "But it looks like the distance is about to be abolished."

She grabbed the keys from Devin's mouth and reached her hand through the bars. She opened the door and did the same for Karl. Before the rearick even had time to swing the gate open, she was inside Hadley's cage, kneeling by his side. With a glance over her shoulder, she said to Karl, "We're right behind you, but he's not gonna be much use. You're going to have to figure out how to deal with the guards."

"I've got just the thing." Karl turned for the hall, grabbing his warhammer along the way. "Good to have ye back," he snorted, eyeing his weapon.

Leaving the jail room behind, Karl figured out what was making so much noise. One of the guards was leaning his knee on the chest of some helpless sap who was lying flat on the floor. The guard had a freakishly large fist raised in the air.

"Why don't ya try that out on someone standin' upright?" Karl said, holding the hammer out in front of him.

Taking one look at the rearick, the guard glanced toward the door.

"I can throw her pretty damned well." He tilted his hammer in the guard's direction. "You'll not make it, son. Let's go man to man."

The man stood, rubbing his hands to get ready for combat.

"Parker?" Karl said, finally seeing the target of the man's blows.

Looking up, Parker wheezed, "All right, Karl. Your turn. I think he's had enough from me." And then his head went slack and dropped back to the floor.

"Aye, now it's personal, you freakish twat." Karl narrowed his eyes. "Come on!"

"I've never seen a child with such a thick beard before," the man said in a gravelly voice. "I'll go easy on you, son." A sneer cut across his face as he sprung in Karl's direction.

The guard snapped a right hook so fast, Karl had no time to react. It caught him on the chin and pain exploded beneath his beard. As the man attempted to follow with another, Karl dodged left, and drew the butt of the hammer up into the guy's gut.

With an "*ooph*," the guard doubled over.

In the small space, he couldn't get much momentum, but Karl managed to swing his hammer into the guard's knee, dropping the man to the floor next to Parker. Eyes wide, Karl drew the hammer back over his head for the finishing blow.

"No!" Laurel shouted as she watched the man writhe in pain.

Karl paused. "No, what?"

Shaking her head, she muttered, "Doesn't feel right. Just lock him up."

"Scheisse, is this a druid thing?"

"Protecting life? As far as I can tell it's just a decency thing." She nodded to the guard. "This guy was just doing his job. Let's lock him up."

Karl snorted, and slung his hammer to his hip. "Alright, lass, but if this douche ends up killin' me in my sleep some night, you'll have to live with that."

She raised her brows. "I think I can handle it. A lot more rearick where you came from."

Karl dragged the guard to the cell and shut the door. Rapping his knuckles on the metal, Karl got the man's attention. "Just be glad Princess Pinecone was with me. If not, this would have ended differently."

Between gasps, the man groaned, "We will get the boy back."

"Boy?"

Before he could answer, the guard passed out from the pain.

"Let's get the hell outta here," Karl said as he pulled Parker to his feet.

Hadley was leaning against the wall, still woozy.

"What's with him?" Parker asked, rubbing his face, which was starting to swell.

"Rock to the head," Karl said. "Shame to lose his only asset."

"Still have my good looks," Hadley said, forcing a smile. "Can we get out of here now? I never thought I'd say this, but I just want to get back to the ship."

Parker and the others agreed. "Follow me down the stairs. Once we get through the back door, there's an alley that will dump us at the base of the hill. If all goes well, we should be able to get out of here as easily as I got in."

Karl snorted, "Aye, mate. What could possibly go wrong?"

His head pounded with each beat of his heart as Hadley took the steps behind Parker. Nothing was worse for a mystic than a blow to the head, and if he were going to be useful, he'd need to push away the pain. Focus. Laurel's magic had helped, at least a bit, but the thunderstorm in his head remained.

"Stay close," Parker whispered, standing at the closed door that opened out into the village. "When I came in, there were only a few folks milling around."

Hadley nodded, but he was hardly listening to the Arcadian. Instead, he tried to quell the pain between his ears enough to reach out to Hannah, let her know their situation. But it seemed no use. The distraction was too great. He needed true rest, healing from the physical trauma that interrupted his state of mind.

The connection between the physical and mental was something that few non-mystics understood, and just as few mystics paid much attention to. Legend had it that the connection between one's physical nature and mental state was one of the reasons that the mystics brew had to be developed so carefully. A hangover or even a groggy haze would interrupt their mental connection with the world around them and with others.

A rock to the head would do even worse.

"Ready?" Parker whispered to his friends behind him. They all nodded as Parker reached for the door. "Remember. Stay quiet. Stay low. We'll be out of here before you know it."

He pushed the door open, sun blinding them all for a moment. As their eyes adjusted, Karl was the first to speak. "Scheisse. Hell of an escape, kid."

The early evening air was still and quiet, but it was nothing compared to the stillness that sat between the guards and the group from the Arcadian valley. Tension grew in the distance between them, but that silence was broken by something more terrifying—the sound of footsteps.

One after another, people filed in from all directions from the small village. Men, women, and children—each with their long, defined arms, and stretched out legs—took their positions behind the guards.

"Looks like the whole damned place came out to welcome us," Laurel said with a giggle. "Guess we're pretty important or something."

"Gonna go with *or something*," Karl exhaled, gripping his hammer tightly. "Seems we should have lined up some back up." His eyes cut across the crowd which numbered in the dozens. "Like a whole bloody army."

Parker turned his staff for the sky, blasting three clear rounds over the quiet village. "We got an army of one, who rides on the back of a dragon!"

Just as he shot, the guards advanced. Some of them spun long ropes with rocks attached to either side, but most of them simply gripped their big hands into massive balls. Hadley could only assume they were palming rocks—the people's weapon of choice.

"No time to wait on dragons," Karl grunted. He lifted his hammer over his head and let loose a spine-chilling bellow into the air. Stepping up, a group of six or eight were on him, but the rearick moved with the experience of a seasoned veteran. Bodies flew in every direction as Parker turned to the north and advanced with his staff on an oncoming group.

Shit, Hadley thought, gripping his head. The mystic wasn't terrible in martial combat, but without his mind working properly, he'd be more of a liability than anything. He stepped back toward the building and slunk to the ground. He had to get control. Looking up at Laurel, she gave him a nod. The druid understood connection, even if not the same kind. She would try to give him time.

But would it be enough?

Devin jumped from her shoulder and crouched by her side. She pulled out her rope blade and began swinging it playfully, as though this was all a game.

Hadley smiled. With people like her on his side, he'd be just fine.

The still night was shattered as three bright bolts of power rocketed through the air. It was Parker's signal, and Hannah wasted no time responding. She lept onto Sal's back, waking him from what appeared to be a pleasant dream.

She gave him a quick kick with her heel, yelling, "Time to stop sunbathing, Sal. Our friends need us."

Sal growled low, then flapped his wings, sending them airborne.

Hannah leaned in, holding her head against her dragon's neck as her hair twisted in the wind. Sal's speed was impressive, and they cleared the distance to the village in seconds. A wave of long-armed villagers swept down upon her friends, who were fighting hand to hand to hold them back. They were losing ground by the minute.

"There," she shouted, pointing to another group of soldiers coming to join the battle.

Sal plummeted like a meteor, coming in low from behind them. At the last second before impact, he pulled up and let out a roar that would terrify the most courageous warrior.

The group hit the ground as the dragon swept over them and banked into a turn. From the back of her flying steed, Hannah could see eyes go wide in terror. People ran in every direction as a creature of myth flew back for another attack.

Coming in more slowly this time, Hannah gave Sal a slap on the side. "Happy hunting," she said, as she pushed off his back. Hitting the ground in a well-practiced roll, she was on her feet, dagger drawn, and ready for battle.

A group of ten ran in from her left. She swiped her hand before her, making a wall of power as if to shield her from their attack. But, instead of a typical defensive field, she shoved both hands forward, pushing the shield in their direction. It bulldozed the group, sending a mass of arms and legs falling in every direction.

Her eyes cut to the battle going on in front of the large building.

Karl was knocking down villagers one after another with his hammer. Each time he dropped one, another engaged. His eyes were resolved, and she knew he could keep it up until the Matriarch herself returned.

Off to the edge, Parker was doing much the same. He was a force to reckon with as his spear spun left and right, keeping the villagers at a distance. They counterattacked with pairs of rocks on ropes, and he narrowly dodged each one.

She cut off toward Laurel. The girl druid was working every advantage she had. A group of villagers were already bound by roots that Laurel had beckoned from underneath, and she was taking care of the rest with her rope blade. But it was the figure she protected that Hannah was most concerned with.

Hadley sat, legs crossed beneath him. His eyes were closed, and Hannah knew he was trying to work. She considered reaching out to him with her mind, but thought it would only distract him from whatever it was he had planned.

Instead, Hannah rushed into an oncoming horde, which were flanking Laurel and Hadley. She ran in hard, lobbing fireballs, large enough to do damage, small enough not to make her energy wane too quickly as she went.

"Aye, what took you so long!" Karl yelled as he ducked a villager's attack and tossed the man over his back.

"Figured you could use the exercise," Hannah shouted back as she directed her magic toward an incoming rock the size of Sal's head. The stone shattered into dust. "After all, it only took you like thirty seconds to get captured down here."

"Bullocks. I would have been fine on my own. It's those kids— they're slowing me down."

Hannah looked at Laurel who sent a half-dozen armed villagers running in fear as her blade cut through the air. The way she moved, as if the weapon were an extension of her body, was frighteningly impressive.

"Somehow, I find it hard to believe that she held you back," Hannah said.

Distracted for a moment, Hannah didn't see the woman charging her until it was too late. She tried to raise her hands in defense, but before the woman could crush her head in with a rock, two large, clawed feet descended from above. Sal grabbed the woman by the shoulders and shot into the air. Hannah laughed as she watched the dragon drop her through a thatched roof.

Despite the impressive display of power her friends were showing off, the villagers would not stop. They came at them again, bleeding and bruised, but undeterred.

"Uh, Hannah, I think we're gonna need a new strategy here," Parker shouted as he and a man a foot taller than him grappled over his spear. Parker fell over backward, bringing the man with him, but then he lifted his feet and launched the man into the wall behind him.

Parker was right. Her friends had managed to avoid major injury so far, but it was only a matter of time before they were brought down.

So, Hannah decided to end it.

She closed her eyes, summoning all the power within her. Her hands crossed in front of her, she channeled her energy into a large ball of blue flame.

Hannah opened her eyes. The villagers all took a step back in fear, but then sprinted forward. This was the only way. She raised the fire above her head.

Then a voice broke through the noise.

"Everyone stop!"

She turned toward the source and saw Hadley, his eyes perfect white crystals. His hands were raised, and she could feel his words tugging at her heart, as if a wave of calm washed over her. By the look in the other villagers' eyes, she could tell they felt his mystic energy, too.

Everyone stopped what they were doing—all eyes were on Hadley.

"There has been a misunderstanding. We are not your enemies."

Everyone glanced around, villagers and Hannah's crew alike looked confused.

"Tell me," he said, this time his voice softer. "Who is Samet?"

CHAPTER SIX

"Helluva a job back there," Hannah whispered to Hadley as she eased into a chair cut out of a giant log. A dozen or so chairs just like it were arranged in a circle around a fire.

She was impressed with his work. Even with the head injury, he was able to broker a temporary ceasefire between Hannah's team and the Baseeki—the strangely limbed people who had "welcomed" them to their village. It was equally a testament to his personality and his power.

Now, it was on Hannah and him to ensure the ceasefire remained in effect long enough for her and her friends to get the hell out of here.

"So," she said. "Got any more tricks up your sleeve? Was there some sort of negotiation training you went through back in the temple?"

Hadley grunted noncommittally and kept his eyes locked on the fire. His face was drawn and gaunt. She hadn't seen him like this before, and she was worried, that the rock that hit him knocked a few screws loose.

She reached over and placed her hand on his back. Hadley's body trembled beneath her touch, showing just how much the events of the day had sapped him. Although she was tired also, and there was no telling what was in store, she couldn't stand to see him like that.

Pushing aside all of the thoughts of Lilith, the Coming Darkness, the villagers, and whatever else, she focused only on her friend. Her eyes flashed red as she pushed her power into him, hoping that it might carry him through to some true rest.

Instantly, his face regained some color and he sat up a little straighter. Turning, he muttered, "Thanks for the pick me up. You wouldn't want to rub my feet, would you?"

Hannah laughed, glad that her friend was back. "Let's leave the rest of your healing up to time and nature."

Karl, Laurel, and Parker stood behind them. The rest of the wooden seats were filled with villagers, mostly older, wizened-looking characters with a few younger folks mixed in. Behind them stood rows of villagers gathered to hear what was going on and what would happen with the foreigners.

Most of them were fixated on Sal. He had been chasing around a group of squealing children, but their parents put a stop to that pretty fast. Without anything else to do, he laid his head on his front claws and stared at the fire like he was bored.

The village council rose as an ancient man with hair halfway down his back approached. Hannah followed suit and lifted Hadley out of his chair as well. One pace behind the man walked a woman, who looked to be in her thirties. She had a subtle kind of beauty, but there was fire in her eyes. Something about her reminded Hannah of Amelia, but she couldn't place what.

When the old man sat, the group followed suit. He sat in silence, eyes moving around the circle, slowing when he got to Hannah and Hadley. She thought his face looked kind, with it's bushy salt and pepper brows, thin beard, and a hooked nose. Keeping her eyes on him, she waited for a smile, but it never came.

"As is our custom, I welcome our visitors in the names of the Great Mother and Father and offer our hospitality."

"If that's their hospitality, I'd hate to see their rudeness." Karl grumbled under his breath. Hannah shot him a look over her shoulder, and he promptly shut his mouth.

The old man's eyes cut to the rearick; he sized him up but ignored his grumble. "Now, it seems we have some things to discuss, but first a proper introduction." His eyes fell on Hannah, as if he knew she was their leader. "Who the hell are you, and what are you doing here in Baseek?"

Hannah stood. "Sir…"

"You can call me Sef," he said, a hint of a smile danced on his lips.

"Sef, I am Hannah of Arcadia, and these are my companions." She paused, realizing that she was uncertain if the time called for the truth or if lying was the better course of action. She chose someplace in between. "We are on a quest to the northeast."

Sef tilted his head in thought and then laughed. "Damned if anyone would want to go anyplace north of here. What is this quest?"

Suddenly, she wished Ezekiel were with her. The story she carried about the Oracle was outlandish, and she wasn't sure how it would play with these strangers. "There is a woman there that we wish to visit, an ancient and wise woman. We are hoping she will have some answers about the future of Arcadia."

The old man nodded. He was patient—too patient. The silence was maddening. Hannah gave up on waiting and recounted an abbreviated version of the story about Arcadia and Adrien, how the people had overcome his tyranny and were working to rebuild the city. All of the villagers leaned in as they listened, and Hannah wished she could create holograms to enhance her tale.

"And what might the wisdom of an old woman of the North add to the restoration of Arcadia?"

She froze again, mind racing. "Well, you see, Sef... Our hope is not just for the city, but for all of the Arcadian Valley. Perhaps all of Irth. Our hope is to gain counsel on how the regions of Irth might be once again united, like in the days before the Madness."

The old man laughed, and the others, after a pause, joined in. "Well, I guess the Arcadian Valley is still rife with fairy tales. People have never been united, never will be. Our region is living proof of that. I guess that is why we have you here."

"Tell me more." Hannah sat and waited, hoping to get out of the interrogation seat.

He nodded and rubbed the coarse hair on his cheeks. "Did they tell you why you're here? Why we took your friends into custody?"

"Not exactly." She glanced over at Hadley who gave her a slight nod. "I assume it has something to do with Samet."

She paused again and tried to read Sef's face. It softened, his eyes grew glassy. With a nod, he said, "It does indeed. But I can tell, you don't know what that means, do you?"

"I wouldn't be so fast with that judgment, Sef," the woman who had accompanied him in broke her silence and hissed into the circle. The firelight danced in her eyes as she stared at Hannah. "If they know his name, then they know his worth. It's proof that they are somehow involved with all this—as if their strange powers weren't reason enough for suspicion."

"Hush, Vatan," the chief said, while raising a finger to silence her. "Give our guests a chance to explain themselves."

Hannah could tell he was smart, testing the waters. The woman, Vatan, sitting to his right wasn't as patient as the old man. Patience is a product of years, and she only had a few more than Hannah under her belt.

Placing her hands in her lap, Hannah closed her eyes for a moment, so as not to show her red glowing eyes as she tried to enter the man's mind. He was not barring her, but she still could not make out much—all she found was a deep and mournful grief.

Opening her eyes again, she said, "I don't know who Samet is. But I know loss when I see it. Before I came upon my companions here, I lived with my father and brother. They were both taken from me by the tyranny of a wicked man and those who followed him. I sense that you also have lost someone. You've lost Samet."

Finally, the smile she hoped for moments ago spread on his face, but this smile was contrasted by the sorrow that filled his eyes. "Indeed. You are correct. I have also lost, lost all that remains dear to me. Samet is my son." Eyes dipping to the dirt ground, he crossed his long lanky arms over his chest and exhaled slowly, as if to gain his composure in front of the foreigners.

After a moment, he looked back at Hannah. "Violence is everywhere indeed, and we outside of the Arcadian Valley are not immune to it. We, the Baseeki, have lived here for generations. Most of our ancestors founded this community sometime during the mad times. Like people the world over, they did what they had to do to survive, often taking to the rocks," he nodded to the south, "or the sea, but they never gave up on this spot, their home."

Hannah listened intently, she could feel Hadley beside her, taking in the words. He, too, understood the connection to place, as did Laurel and Karl. And while life in the Boulevard wore her down, she still felt some sort of affinity for the only place she had ever called home.

"But not all are good on this stretch of land," Sef continued. "There are tribes on the other side of the mountains. We used to be at peace with them..." he stopped and looked at the woman beside him. "But recently they have been giving us some problems. Then there are the roamers."

"Remnant?" Hannah asked in a hush.

The chief's eyes narrowed. "I do not know this word."

"That's what we call the creatures who remain from the Age of Madness. The descendants of the ones who never fully recovered when the Madness fell. They are stuck between man and animal. Desiring nothing more than to eat, sleep, and screw, they wander our lands ravaging anything they come across."

"Ah, you mean the kilgin. At least that is what we call them here." He shook his head and shifted in his seat. "They can be found near Baseek, but we have learned how to deal with them. Our people keep watch from the cliffs. Even the kilgin know that our aim is true, and the Mother has given us the means to defend ourselves." He held up his long arms in display. His hands were huge wrinkly masses, but they clearly retained their strength. "No, the roamers may be wicked, but they are not unwise. They are human enough, traveling in large numbers throughout the region. For some time, we thought they wanted our land, to settle in our houses. But their motivation is, well, perhaps baser. It seems they only want to sow confusion and fear, which makes their pillaging that much easier."

Parker leaned forward. "And how does your son fit into all of this?"

The chief sighed. "I don't know. But yesterday, he was hunting in the forest with several of the guard. They never returned. I sent my men searching, which is when they stumbled across you and your companions here. My son wouldn't just disappear, not unless something terrible had happened."

"And you believe these roamers took Samet?" Hadley asked.

Sef glanced at the woman behind him and then back to Hannah and the others. "No. I do not. That would be the simple answer, but the truth is seldom so simple, except in children's stories." A few snickers arose from the audience. "I mentioned another tribe, Kofken. They settled east of here, on the coast. For years, Kofken and Baseek have lived in harmony. Trade, common defense against outsiders, even intermarriage from time to time.

But we have begun to doubt their good intentions toward us." He glanced to the woman on his right hand, and she nodded her affirmation.

"And then you all showed up. I don't know what this means. You could be hired kidnappers from Kofken or the roamers. Or you could represent some other threat. Or it could just be a coincidence."

Murmurs arose from behind the chief and his council. Clearly, some were in affirmation of his suspicion, but others doubted.

Sef raised a hand, and the group grew silent.

He's a good man, Hannah heard Hadley say in his head. *His thoughts are a bit wild, but it is because he is distraught.*

She nodded, reaching a decision. "Or maybe it is fate. Maybe we were brought here to help you, to help find your son."

He smiled. "Help us? Half of my village believes you are the cause of our woes. I am impressed by your courage, but the boldness of youth often ends in peril. What makes you believe that you and your friends are able to make a difference in our plight? How can I know this isn't just another trick?"

Looking back at her friends, Parker gave her a wink. "We are fighters, but we also have more than our fair share of power. Some of your people caught a glimpse of what we can do even today."

She raised her hands in front of her chest, and moved them around, as if smoothing them on an invisible orb floating in the air. Her eyes glowed bright red, making the campfire pale in comparison. A bright yellow ball appeared before her. Hannah pushed her hands together in a clap, and the orb burst in a million tiny balls of light, each floating around like fireflies before scurrying off into the surrounding trees.

The old man laughed. "Power indeed. But it takes more than a trick like that to mount a rescue."

"I have more. And my colleagues possess other types of magic.

Instead of fighting us, or locking us away in some dungeon, use the power fate has dropped in your lap. Send us with the best of your guard. We will find your son."

The chief opened his mouth to speak, but Vatan cut him off. "Sef, let us not be fools. We do not know her," she said pointing at Hannah. "You trust the guiles of a witch over the strength of your own? How do we not know that they are the evil which has crept in? Some other evil from an unknown land? You have heard her tale. They want to sneak off with our best fighters so they can kill them in the woods." She paused and scanned the group. "I bet they are mercenaries hired by Kofken."

"Aye, lass, if I were hired to do a job," Karl snorted, "ye'd all be dead on the ground already." His knuckles were white, wrapped on the shaft of his hammer.

A man, taller than anyone Hannah had ever seen stepped out of the shadows and between Sef and the Arcadians. His arms were massive, and his fist were like giant baskets. The guard's face was resigned, showing neither passion nor anger. "I would like to see you try, little man."

"Stand down, Dardanus," Sef said. The man immediately bowed, and then stepped back out of the circle. Hannah was glad the chief acted as he did. She for one had no interest in fighting a person that size.

"You must forgive, Vatan," Sef continued. "She and Samet were close; he was like a brother to her." He paused choosing his words. "But… I must admit, it is hard to trust in the words of a stranger, especially when we simply do not know the truth."

Hannah shifted in the wooden seat. "You're a cautious man, and I respect that. But your son is gone—caution isn't really an option right now. But trust is. If you knew the truth, then there would be no need for trust. Trust can only happen when there are doubts. But… I have an idea that might help us earn your trust."

"Speak freely."

"My friend Laurel and I will go with your best guards. Together we will find your son. You can keep our men here in our stead as a guarantee of our return. Two young women couldn't pose much of a threat, but it would give us a chance to prove ourselves."

"Scheisse, Hannah—" Karl grunted, but he fell silent when his leader shot him a steely glare.

The old man laughed. "Something tells me you and the other fair magician are more of a threat then all of the men combined. But, I will take your deal."

"Sef—" The woman, Vatan, placed her hand on the chief's shoulder, but he silenced her with a shake of his head.

"My decision is final. Return with my son, and you shall have my eternal gratitude, along with whatever help my village can offer. But if you fail, or we find you to be false, your friends lives will be forfeit."

Hannah paused for a moment, not happy with any ultimatum that put her friends in jeopardy. But Parker placed his hand on her shoulder, and she could feel Hadley's affirmation. She turned to look at Karl, who still looked like he wanted to finish the fight. Vatan and him were trying to burn holes in each other with their eyes.

"What do you think, Karl?"

Finally, he sighed, and gave her a smile. "Scheisse. I'd place my money on you and the beansprout any day." He then leaned in close and whispered to her. "That chief is alright, but I don't trust these people. Keep yer eyes open, you hear me?"

She nodded, then turned back to Sef. Crossing over to him, she offered her hand to seal the deal.

Dardanus, the head guard, motioned to Sal, laying lazily by the fire. "And what about that thing?"

Hannah grinned. "Trust me—he would make for a horrible house guest. But I actually have a job for him, if you would allow me."

The sun had set hours ago, but Gregory still stood on the deck of the *Unlawful*, waiting for his friends to signal their return. Nerves were getting the best of him, so he set about checking every technical piece of their flying machine, and then checking them twice. His father's handiwork still amazed him, but over the course of several weeks, he made modifications that improved upon the man's mastery.

He respliced a rope connected to the bow, more for the sake of distraction than necessity.

Gregory, Hannah said in his mind. He jumped, as he always did.

Months had passed since they had first met in the Arcadian Academy, since she tried to teach him magic. Still never really taking to physical magic, they soon found he had some affinity for the mystical arts. Hannah was convinced that it had to do with his brilliance. While he still couldn't conjure images or read minds, he and Hannah could connect mentally. He was convinced it had to do with their friendship.

Where are you? He concentrated harder than ever to reply.

No time to explain. Laurel and the rest of them are safe, but we're going to be down here for a while longer. Keep the boat safe, and DO NOT disturb Ezekiel.

He swallowed hard, thinking of being alone on the ship. Ezekiel hadn't emerged from his room in hours—and there was no telling how long he'd be in there. The physics of it still confused him, but Gregory imagined the kind of long distance connection Ezekiel was trying to achieve took prodigious amounts of energy and focus.

And what if we're...

Gregory, Hannah interrupted, *you're a hundred feet in the air. You should be fine. But... Just in case, I'm sending your favorite body guard.*

No sooner than Hannah finished speaking in his head, did the rushing sound of a mighty wind rise up around him. Sal slammed to the deck and clawed at its boards, pulling himself to a sudden stop at Gregory's feet.

"Great," Gregory said to himself. "And who will protect me from this damned thing?"

CHAPTER SEVEN

Sunlight cut through a gap in the curtains and onto the bed. Hannah ran a finger along the long seam of the mattress, impressed by the villager's craftsmanship. Not only well constructed, but the borrowed bed was more comfortable than the one she had slept in at the mystic's temple. On arrival, she had assumed that the simple nature of the tribe in Baseek meant they were primitive, but evidently that was not the case. Although their village was downright puny in comparison to Arcadia, the Baseeki were nevertheless gifted in construction of all kinds.

Stretching, she rolled out of her bed and nudged Laurel. The girl scrunched her nose and rolled back on her opposite side. "Stop dreaming of Gregory and get your ass out of bed."

Without moving the rest of her body, Laurel raised an arm. "Look, I'm doing magic. I'm making this grow." As she spoke, her middle finger slowly extended toward the sky. Hannah laughed, endeared by the druid and her favorite hand gesture.

"Come on. We gotta go save a prince."

As Laurel stumbled out of her bed, Hannah packed the few things she had brought down from the ship and turned to find a leather vest waiting for her. She held it up, admiring its lapped seams.

"He had it made for you," a voice interrupted her from the open door. "My aunt stayed up all night to get it done before dawn."

Hannah turned to find Vatan standing in the doorway. "It's beautiful."

The woman stepped into the room. "I'll let auntie know. I hope you bring it back in one piece."

The woman smiled, which didn't quite set Hannah at ease. Judging from the events of the previous night, she surmised that Vatan wasn't a fan of the Arcadians, and she certainly didn't trust them. But Hannah couldn't blame her. She would feel the same if a group of warriors and magicians rolled into her town after her brother had been kidnapped.

"About last night," Vatan said.

Hannah stepped forward and extended her hand, which Vatan took in her own. "No worries. You were right to be suspicious, and, frankly, we can be a pretty frightening lot—when we're in the mood."

Vatan's mouth turned in a crooked grin. "I can believe that."

"But it's good to have the scary on your side—and we're on your village's side. We *will* bring Samet back."

The woman's eyes hit the ground, and when they leveled back on Hannah's, they were glassy. With a blink, two large tears dropped, rolling down her chin. She quickly wiped them away. "You must think I'm just some dumb girl."

"No." Hannah placed a hand on her shoulder. "My brother..." Her throat grew tight. "Let's just say I know a piece of what you're going through."

Vatan thanked her and gave Laurel a tiny wave. "Good luck, you two. You find Samet, and I'll make sure your friends are in good hands."

"Seems nice," Laurel said after she had left the room.

Hannah's eyes were still on the doorway, suddenly very worried for her friends' safety. "Yeah. A little too nice. That's what worries me."

Laurel nodded. "A tiger doesn't change its stripes overnight."

"Yeah. I... wait." Hannah raised an eyebrow. "I thought tigers couldn't change their stripes at all."

The druid smiled. "We need to start working on your nature magic. There's a lot you don't know."

———

Having finished breakfast, Hannah and Laurel were allowed one last chance to visit the others. They stood in the prison room on opposite sides of the bars.

"You sure you're going to be OK in here?" Hannah asked. She addressed it to everyone, but she was staring at Parker.

"I'm gonna be great," Karl shouted. He had a large mug of something dark in his hand. It seemed Sef was keeping his promise about taking care of them. "No worries at all. I've got a good drink, a comfy bed, and nothin' to do. It's like a vacation. I've always wanted me one of those. And ya know the best part? No bloody airship. So, ya just take a nice, *long* time finding Prince Twat."

Hannah smiled. "Sounds good, rearick. Just make sure you're sober enough to walk when we get back. I am not carrying you back to the ship."

"Aye aye, captain." He raised his glass in salute, spilling half of it.

"We'll be fine," Parker said. "Don't worry about us, just worry about getting back here safely."

"Preferably with a prince or two on your arm," Hadley winked. "Because I'd rather not see what the Baseeki do to liars."

She nodded. "I'll find him. And if not, well, it's been nice knowing ya. I'll write to you from wherever the Oracle lives."

"I'd cherish them forever," the mystic said.

Hannah couldn't be sure, but she thought she saw Parker's eyes roll. She gave him a lingering pat on the hand, then turned to leave.

Looking back, she said, "While I'm gone, keep an eye out for that Vatan woman. She stopped by this morning and was a little too forceful in her performance of a caring person. She wants something, I just don't know what."

Karl yelled from his cot. "She's probably just interested in my stunnin' good looks. Ha!"

Before Hannah could think of a reply, Laurel grabbed her by the arm and pulled her toward the door. "Come on, come on. Enough of this sap. Let's get to the action." The druid was bouncing on her toes, clearly ready to be back in the woods.

"Don't worry," Hannah said. "I have a feeling that before this is done, we'll get to see plenty of action."

Hannah and Laurel walked toward the edge of the village, the same spot where Parker had snuck in. Sef and Vatan stood before them, a dozen men behind.

"Might the Mother and Father be gracious on your journey," Sef said. "My gratitude goes with you, but do not bring my fury with deceit."

"You won't be disappointed," Hannah said.

Sef looked past her and waved to the group of guards. Dardanus stepped forward. He looked even larger in the light of the day. He stood more than three feet taller than Hannah, dark, black hair fell to his shoulders. He was strikingly handsome—despite his weirdly proportioned body. His feet were even larger than his hands, and on top of his long, lean legs, Hannah couldn't help but think of him like a giant walking frog.

Despite their thin nature, it was clear that the Baseeki's arms and legs were built like iron.

Sef reached up and placed a hand on Dardanus's broad shoulder, eyes still on Hannah. "I'm sending my best eight with you. They are my personal guard, not only strong, but also loyal. Dardanus here will be invaluable on the search and rescue."

"Good to know," Hannah smiled tentatively. "And S, since I'm going after your son, do me a favor, will you?"

"What is it, Arcadian?"

"Don't be a dick to the guys you have in lock up. I know you don't trust us yet, but as long as they are out of play, treat them well. They're good men, all three of them."

Sef flushed, and she could tell he was almost ashamed of the deal they had worked out. In Hannah's estimation, he was indeed a good man, attempting to do right by his people. The precaution of locking up Parker, Hadley, and Karl was the sensible option— and she had been the one to suggest it.

"Other than the bars, I will care for them as if they were one of my own... Unless, of course, you turn on us. Then they will have all of the righteous justice of Baseek turned on them."

The tone of his voice sent a chill through her, and she knew he would make good on his promise.

Without another word, Dardanus and his men took to the hill. Hannah and Laurel had nothing to do but follow suit.

They walked the first mile toward the summit in silence, and for a moment, Hannah wondered if she had stepped into a trap. She cursed herself and considered what line of action Ezekiel would have taken. But he wasn't here, and all she could do was to trust her instincts and follow Dardanus's lead.

By the top, she and Laurel were breathing heavy. Weeks on the ship had done nothing for their fitness, even with semi-regular training sessions with the rearick. But the others, the guards from Baseek, looked as if they had been lounging in the sun all day. Their home, where the steep rocky crags met the ocean, had shaped them for peak health and fitness. Hannah knew if they wanted to finish her and the druid off, now would be their best bet.

They didn't. Instead, the men pulled out skins filled with deliciously sweet water and passed them around, not skipping the new members of their party.

Hannah decided to break the silence. "Let me ask you a question, Big D. Sef mentioned Baseeki justice. What exactly does that entail?"

The big man shrugged. "Simple. We tie boulders to the feet of the accused and throw them from the cliffs. Let the sea decide who is guilty."

Hannah had a brief mental image of Parker sinking to his death. She tried her best to shake it away.

"Now, let me ask you a question, Arcadian," Dardanus said, looking into the sky. "What is it? Some sort of hovering cart or something?"

The other men shared his gaze, which was directed at the airship, floating low enough to make out the shape of its hull.

"Yeah. Something like that. It's an airship, I guess. We call it the *Unlawful*—kind of an inside joke. As far as I know, it's the only one of its kind."

Dardanus's stern face softened a little. "But how does it stay up there like that? Why doesn't it crash down on our heads?"

Hannah grabbed the skin of water from another guard and soothed her burning throat with the cool drink. She then took some time to tell them the short story about Adrien and Arcadia, and about the way he built the ship with the intention of taking over all of Irth. She closed the story with his final demise, taking time to really make the part about his death ring in their ears.

"I imagine," he replied, "that if you didn't kill your former ruler, his ship would have drifted over us sometime anyway."

Hannah nodded. She hadn't thought about it before, but, if they hadn't halted the maniac's devices, it was very likely that after taking Cella, he may have turned the ship east toward Baseek, leveling every little village between Arcadia and the hill they stood on.

Hannah shrugged. "Probably true. Who knows? It's a big world, bigger than any of us know. But I imagine if all went according to plan, he would have kept rolling. Those who submitted he would have squeezed for anything of value. Those who resisted would have been razed to the ground.The ship has some powerful weaponry."

Shading his eyes with his hand, Dardanus narrowed his gaze, inspecting the underside of the ship. "Those two things that look like mini tree trunks?"

"Mmm, hmm."

"Damn. If I can see them from here, they must be enormous."

Hannah watched his face change. "Big enough to destroy my quarter of Arcadia in under thirty seconds. Killed half the people I knew in the process."

His eyes drifted down from the airship and back to Hannah. "Guess if you meant us ill, you wouldn't need to walk into Baseek and fight us hand to hand."

A tiny grin formed on her face. "No. I don't expect we would have. Unless, of course, we decided we just couldn't live without those tiny huts on the water. I mean, it is a pretty nice piece of property you have there."

For the first time in Hannah's hearing, Dardanus laughed, and it was a hearty one. "Yeah," he said, getting control of his laughter. "I guess at least from a hundred feet up, they wouldn't seem like much, would they?"

"I mean no offense, Dard. That was a damned nice bed I slept in, but we flew over hundreds of castles and all kinds of shit that I couldn't explain what it was or how it was built. We don't want anything from you and yours. Came down to get some supplies, and we kind of fell into this."

"Like a big pile of horseshite."

Hannah smiled. "Nah. I don't believe in destiny or fate—although they make for pretty words around the campfire. Don't tell anyone, but I'm still not even sure about how I feel about the Matriarch and the Patriarch. But for some reason, I do believe we're here for a reason. Not sure how to explain that with all I just said. So, what do you say we go make my transcendent destiny complete?"

"Sounds good to me." He made the sign of a circle over his head, and the men fell in behind him. Only this time, Hannah stayed in the front with Dardanus. Laurel wandered at her own pace, taking in the land around her. Now that she was out of her cage, she was loving every minute of this little trip.

CHAPTER EIGHT

They stayed atop the ridgeline for several hours, moving to the east. Rocks and boulders were strewn along the ground as they approach the cliffs that stood out from the hills. Hannah and Laurel were swift and passed over them with relative ease. But compared to the men from Baseek, they were like children just learning to walk. It was as if the men got more agile when there were obstacles to be crossed.

As the ground smoothed out for a few hundred yards, Hannah walked in silence, taking in the world around her. While every-thing—the hills, trees, dirt, and plants—were something like those in her homeland, it wasn't the same. Her eyes combed the rocks, seeing how they were different than the cliffs of the Heights,

Her head jerked ninety degrees when she heard a snap down in the tree line.

Watching for movement, she saw none. She pushed away her thoughts and tried to swipe the area with her mind, looking for some sign of other sentient beings. Nothing.

"What is it?" Dardanus asked, pulling up beside her.

"It's just… Well, nothing. Just got spooked."

He grinned. "A lot out here to spook ya, especially after dark. Let's keep the pace up."

Falling in beside him, she asked, "Where we heading to, anyway?"

"There's a spot up there." He pointed to the cliffs, which appeared seamless to her untrained eye. "A place where there is a break in the rocks. There's a patch of flat land before the cliffs rise again. It's really quite beautiful. I used to go there when I was a kid to camp out. Guess it's a bit of a Baseeki tradition, because Vatan told us that Samet would hike up there often by himself. A little getaway, just like it was for me. Thought we should see what we might find there."

Hannah nodded and looked back over her shoulder for any movement in the trees behind them, but it seemed they were alone.

"Sounds like a pretty good life," she said as they hit another pile of rocks on their approach to the cliffs.

Her breathing got heavier, while Dardanus spoke as if out for a leisurely walk. "Yeah. It has been. Until recently."

"What's happened?" she wheezed.

"Nothing much has happened. That's the worst part of the whole thing. Most of our problems have included the kilgin or some of the roamers. I'm fine taking these guys and a few other hands to deal with them. But you can't fight words with our fists and rocks."

His earnest words struck her, and she began to suspect that there was more to the guard than brawn and brute strength. She kept silent, hoping he would continue his story.

"People started to talk about the Kofken village and how they wanted what we have. Some folks were even proposing we attack them first."

"You don't believe it, do you?" Hannah asked.

"Hell, I'm related to half those folks. Some by blood, some by marriage. Hard to imagine they would turn on us. But in the center of the heart lies a little piece of darkness, you know? Just depends on whether or not we let it grow... and what we do with it if it does."

Hannah walked in silence for a moment, thinking of her own heart when Will and her father were killed. If it weren't for Ezekiel, she had no idea how she would have directed her passions, and who might have gotten in the way of them. She didn't know if there was darkness in all of them, but she did get a glimpse of her own. The magician helped her turn that darkness to light, the passion to power.

"You still think the stories are shite?"

Dardanus smiled. "I'm not out here because I am one of the sharpest knives in the drawer. All I can do is think as I can." He paused. Hannah wanted to argue, but she allowed him to continue. "Didn't think all those words were worth one shiny shit when a few were speaking them, but, you know, as more and more people were talking about it, and when..."

"Yeah?" Hannah goaded him on.

"Well, when Vatan and Sef actually started to consider the possibility, it became harder to deny. Something happened to Samet"

Dardanus didn't miss a beat as he scrambled up a precarious rock and mantled up over its lip. He reached down and grabbed Hannah's hand, hauling her in like she weighed nothing, then did the same for Laurel.

"So, you think they have him?" Hannah asked as they picked their way through the rocks on the other side.

"Dunno," he said. Then he stopped short and look Hannah dead in the eyes. "Actually, no. No, I don't. I'm going to need more evidence than a shit ton of he said, she said to believe the people of Kofken would stoop so low. It would be like them blaming us of the same."

Hannah walked carefully as rocks shifted beneath each step. Catching a glimpse of Laurel over her shoulder, she saw that the druid walked a bit more lithely. Once she had her footing under-neath her, Hannah said, "Sounds to me like you're a lot sharper than most of the knives I've thrown."

Dardanus flushed a shade of pink and kept his remaining words to himself.

A few more yards down the stony path, the sound of rocks rolling into some brush caught their attention from her right. Hannah spun, as did Dardanus.

"Someone's following us," she said, with more confidence than she had felt before.

Dardanus held up his hand, telling her to stay. She complied, letting the massive man do what he did best. He walked silently across the rocks. From his right hand, hung a rope with two rocks attached, one on either end. She had heard one of the men call them bolas. They swayed back and forth with his stride. It was a simple weapon, but Hannah could only assume he would give a magitech wielding Capitol Guard a run for his money.

Laurel stood by Hannah's side. "Someone is hiding in that brush." She nodded in the direction that Dardanus was walking.

"Girl, how the hell do you know that?"

"Come on," Laurel said with a grin. "It's plants. If there's something I know…"

Hannah held her hand up. "OK, I get it. Another thing you're going to have to show me."

Dardanus stopped and stood tall five yards from the brush where Laurel had pointed. He swung the bolas at his side, which made the gentlest whooshing sound. A slight shake of the shrub, and he launched his weapon.

"The hell!" a shrill voice cried out.

Before it could utter another word, the long right arm of the guard shot into the bush. When he pulled it back, a young girl emerged, held a foot off the ground by Dardanus's big hand. His bola was wrapped around her ankles. Hannah and Laurel rushed to him with the other guards close behind.

The girl kicked in the air, not close enough to Dardanus to make contact. The words coming from her mouth sounded altogether crass, though Hannah couldn't make any of them out. She wondered if she were about to meet someone from Kofken, until she noticed her missing hand.

"Hey, I know you," Hannah said with a smile. "You tried to bash my head in with a rock."

The girl glared at Hannah for a second, then said. "Technically, it was your weird looking friend I was trying to hit."

Hannah laughed, making a mental note to let Parker know how the local woman viewed him.

Letting her drop to the ground, Dardanus shouted at the girl. "The hell you doing out here, Aysa? You should know better, especially now with Samet missing."

She pushed herself to her feet and pulled the hem of her leather vest down toward her belt. She was young, younger than Laurel, but she carried herself like someone twice her age.

"Well, since all of you were busy sitting around the fire talking with the damned visitors, I decided it was time someone went looking for Sam. I'd have found him, too, if you brutes didn't get in my way."

"And what makes you think the enemy wouldn't have gotten you first?"

Aysa, knowing he was right, turned a shade of red. "Sam is a chance worth taking."

Dardanus crossed his arm as he looked down on her. She stood tall, as if trying to appear larger than she was in front of the chief's guard. Stealing a glance at Hannah and Laurel, she said, "And, who the hell are these two anyway?"

Dardanus's face was stern. "They have been commissioned to help me find the son of the chief, by Sef himself. Unlike you, who are here without permission. Now, it's time for you to climb back down the hill to the village and let the adults handle this."

"Like hell I will," she spat at Dardanus, though her eyes were still on Hannah.

Hannah's heart skipped a beat when the girl spoke. She had spunk and fight, two things evidently helpful in situations like these. "Nice to meet you," she interjected. "You know, without getting into a fight."

The girl nodded and turned back to Dardanus, "Send me back. Once I'm beyond the edge of that rock, I'll be off on the chase again. You can't stop me. You want me with you or near you?"

"Ah, damnit, Aysa. Don't do it like this."

"Like what?"

Dardanus shook his head. "For one, Sef will have your ass if you don't get it back to the village."

"And?"

"And I'll kick your ass myself if you get in our way." Dardanus shifted his weight from one foot to another. Evidently, talking Aysa out of the mission was more harrowing to him than hunting down roamers, remnant, or nefarious Kofkens.

Hannah read it all, and she liked it. She liked the girl. Aysa reminded her of a younger version of herself, and she'd be glad to have the girl along for the journey.

"Well, commence with the ass kicking, or get out of my way," the girl spouted. "Either I'm coming with you, or I'm going by myself."

Dardanus grumbled under his breath and paced back and forth. The girl had him by the balls, and they all knew it.

"All right," he said. "But first, you tell me what you know."

Aysa dusted off her hands. "A few days ago, the day that Sam left the village, I was out exploring, when I saw him and his guards.

"More like you were creeping on him, aye, Aysa?" Cal, Dardanus's second in command scoffed.

She turned a shade of pink, but ignored him. "I followed Sam and his men up here. Everything was normal. Sam was hopping from rock to rock like he was a newly freed prisoner, and the guards were walking behind him, muttering about being babysitters when there were more important things to be done. Nothing out of the ordinary."

"That's all you've got?" Dardanus asked. Hannah knew that it was more than nothing, and she knew that he also realized it.

"Well, not quite," the girl continued. "They dropped down into the cleft." She motioned around them. "Down here. I wasn't sure what to do, so I climbed behind that boulder up there. I didn't have a clear view, but I heard…" She trailed off, and silence overtook her.

"Heard what?"

"Well, pretty sure they were arguing."

Dardanus took a step toward the girl. "About what?"

She shrugged. "Not positive. Like I said, I was up there, too far to really hear much of anything. I snuck out of my spot and tried to get closer. When some rocks shifted beneath my feet, one of them saw me. He started yelling, really tearing me a new one, telling me to get my little ass back to the village."

"So, did you?" Hannah asked.

The girl smiled. "Hell no. They aren't the boss of me. I just got out of view again. I… I guess I was worried for him. When all finally went quiet, I walked down in here and found… Nothing."

Dardanus made a "hmph" noise and looked out into the area known as the cleft. "You wait here," he said to Aysa. "Men, spread out. Leave no stone unturned."

Hannah looked at the crew of long limbed men and then over the land that lay before them. She grabbed Dardanus by his arm. "If I might offer a suggestion. 'No stone unturned' would take an eternity. Why not let my friend in there first to scope out the scene?"

He gave her a scowl. "And what would she know about this land that my men wouldn't?"

"Trust me, she's a druid. She'll be able to judge between the natural and unnatural disruptions. And there's another thing."

Dardanus lifted a brow. "Besides her being a master tracker? What's that?"

"She can kind of talk with the plants."

He turned to Laurel. "Is that true?"

"Do you really want a botany lesson right now, or do you want me to see if I can find your prince or whatever?"

"I'm surrounded by children," he replied shaking his head and trying to make sense of these strange women in front of them. "Well, get in there then."

Laurel smiled, kicked off her shoes, and walked barefoot into the area in question.

Watching her go, Dardanus said, "The magic you have is unbelievable—I mean, truly unbelievable. Does everyone in the Arcadian Valley practice magic?"

"Not everyone, but there are a fair number of us, and growing every day. They used to restrict who could use magic and who couldn't... but we took care of that."

"Damn," he grunted. "Strange place your land must be then. And with freakish people—no offense."

"None taken."

Dardanus was still shaking his head when Laurel emerged from the spot in the trees.

"Yeah, there were people here all right," Laurel stated plainly. "Looks like three, maybe four fully grown folks. Another smaller body, probably my size. But I didn't see much indication of violence. Nothing large scale anyway."

"No way those guards would have given in without a fight. If they were attacked, there would be blood."

They all glanced at Aysa. She shrugged. "I'm just telling you what I heard. Didn't see any roamers or Kofkens or anything. Just Baseeki guards arguing. Maybe the roamers snagged Sam without a struggle." Her face turned a little pale. "Or poisoned him."

Hannah thought over the girl's response. She had no reason to be suspicious of her tale, but, on the other hand, she certainly had no reason to trust her either. But something about Samet's disappearance didn't feel right, and scenarios rushed through Hannah's mind.

Why would a prince go missing on his own land, with his own guards? she thought.

"Something's off," she said.

"Agreed," Dardanus replied. "Let's get in there and really scour the area. We'll do it my way this time"

It was evident that the spot in the cleft of rocks was a popular place for the Baseeki to come to. It was worn, and looked as though camps had been set up there for years. In the middle was a clearing, the remnants of a fire circle that looked as if it was often used. Hannah walked the perimeter again as the others combed inside.

Search as she could, nothing seemed odd or out of place. Just a spot in the woods where the kids would get away. Places like this existed all over the world. For her and her brother, it was abandoned houses. For country kids like the Baseeki, it was a secluded spot on the rocks.

"Dardanus," a gruff voice shouted. "Over here. The tiny one found something."

Everyone rushed to the far end of the clearing. Laurel was there, staring at a mark in the bark of a large tree.

"Something hit this," she said. "Something hard. And look, there's some blood."

She stared at it for a second, then placed her hands on the tree. The Baseeki all looked at each other, confused, when she opened her eyes and pointed to a cluster of bushes.

Cal walked over to it and began digging around. "Son of a

bitch," he shouted. "Dardanus, you're gonna want to come see this."

"Here," Cal shouted. He was digging through a bush nearby and pulled out.

Lying behind the bush, like it had been concealed in a hurry, was the dead body of a Baseeki man. His head was crushed in.

"This is Emen," Dardanus said. "One of Samet's guards."

Hannah leaned in to observe the body. "What happened to him?"

"This," Cal said. He rolled the body over and picked up a smooth, ornately carved stone the size of a pear. He handed it to Dardanus.

"Dammit. This is from Kofken alright." He showed it to Hannah. "We Baseeki prefer our bolas, but the Kofken find perfect stones like this and use them in slings. See these markings? That's Kofken craftsmanship. It's exquisite."

Hannah shook her head. "Why the hell would they decorate their rocks if they just chuck them at people?"

"Our people—the Baseeki and the Kofkens—believe anything worth doing is worth doing well. The work of our hands is an act of worship to the Mother and Father, and we'll be damned if we give them something half-assed."

Hannah put out her hand, and he granted the stone for her closer inspection. It was beautiful, but it reminded her of the well-made bed she had slept in the night before.

Hannah stepped into a patch of sunlight and looked more closely. The stone was dark on one side. She scratched it and red flakes came off.

"There's blood on this," she said, looking up at Dardanus.

"That's all the evidence I need," he said through gritted teeth. "We're heading to Kofken."

CHAPTER NINE

Karl lay flat on his back, staring up at the ceiling of their jail cell and whistling an old folk tune from the Heights. A cup of the Baseeki's finest ale was balanced on his belly, and the hue of red his cheeks had turned indicated that it wasn't his first.

He stopped whistling and laughed.

"What's so damned funny?" Parker asked as he paced the cell. They had been returned to the village's rudimentary prison—for their safety, Vatan had assured them. This time, all three of them were locked up in a larger cell. Fine furniture had been moved in along with other creature comforts. Karl was testing to see if the ale was truly all you could drink.

"The tune I been humming," he sighed. "It's an old war tune— well, *after* war tune. The victors would sing it as they marched their arses home. Words are about freedom. Funny thing is, I'm feeling freer now than I have in months."

Parker huffed. "Hannah could be in danger out there."

"Aye, could be, mate. But she also set us up in a good way before she left. I plan on enjoying every damned minute of captivity—on the ground." He took another slug from the mug. "Scheisse, their swill ain't bad either. Ye should sit yer scrawny arse down Parker and get piss drunk with me. Though, I'm 'fraid I'm halfway home." He nodded at Hadley, who sat straight up, legs crossed and eyes closed on his bed. "Or at least go all trancey like our friend over thar. That way ya'd drive me just a little less nuts."

"Something's not right here, Karl." Parker continued to pace. "I can't put my finger on it, but I've got a bad feeling about this whole thing."

"Only thing off is that my little vacation here don't include some fine young rearick on dis here bed with me." Karl laughed to himself. "And I guess the fact that ya blokes would be in here with us, too."

Finishing his cup, he reached back over his head and tapped it on the metal bars. A young porter came over and grabbed it with his long, lanky arms before passing it back through the bars.

"Thanks, kid." He said. "I owe ya one."

The porter returned to his seat in the corner.

"Are you listening, Karl?" Parker nearly shouted.

"Trying not to. Why don't you enjoy our little break in paradise?"

"We gotta get out of here," Parker said in a whisper with his eyes cutting over to the young Baseeki in the corner. "Between the three of us, shouldn't be hard to bust out of here. Sneakily this time. Then we find Hannah… I'm telling you, something is definitely not right here."

"You said that already," Hadley said, breaking his silence. His eyes were open and transitioning back to their normal color. "And if we do break out of here, it's only going to put Hannah in more trouble. If you care for her so much, it's time to trust her. She's a big girl. Hannah can take care of herself."

"Aye," Karl said with a belch as he sat up on his bed.

Ignoring the rearick, Parker glared at Hadley. "You don't have to tell me what Hannah can and can't do. I've known her since we were freaking kids."

Hadley smiled, knowing he was getting under Parker's skin. "Yeah, Park. You're right. You and Hannah are really good friends. I'm sure you'll stay like that for a long time. Good, good friends."

Blood boiling beneath his skin, Parker strode across the cell, ready for attack. He and Hadley had grown as close as brothers, but like brothers, the mystic took jabs at Parker whenever possible. And every insult was about Hannah.

Before he could land a blow, the door to the jailroom squeaked open, a guard with arms down past his knees walked in. "The chief would like to talk with each of you individually. Starting with you." He pointed at Karl.

"How come?" Parker asked.

The kid looked nervous, but Karl laughed. "I'm sure he's just wants to get to know his guests better. Some more Baseeki hospitality."

The rearick laughed again. "Well, as long as the chief knows I been enjoyin' some of his liquid hospitality fer hours," he said, holding up his cup, "this should go just fine."

Karl stumbled to his feet, steadied himself, and then looked over at Hadley. "Aye, and you'll have to finish dat story later kid."

The mystic looked back confused.

"Ya know, the one where you broke out of the whorehouse in the Quarter when the shit hit the fan. Always be ready." He winked and followed the guard out of the jail.

Three steps toward the cockpit, Gregory spun on his heels. Sal stopped short, nearly running into him. "Will you just give me some space?" he shouted at the dragon.

Sal bent low, jaw nearly on the deck and looked up, giving Gregory a few blinks of his beady, black eyes.

Gregory exhaled long and slowly. "I know she told you not

to leave me, but damn it, Sal, don't take everything so literally. I'll be fine. Listen, I gotta land this tub. She's not flying as straight as she should, and I have to check the hull. I'm worried there may have been some damage from the last storm, and if we're going to fly her all the way to Lilith, she's gotta be tiptop."

Sal cocked his head to the side, and Gregory sighed. "I know that might seem a little risky. But everyone else is out there risking their lives—I have to do something. And right now, my only responsibility is this ship. OK, so just, go take a nap or something."

Sal growled in disapproval, then plodded back to mid-deck and curled up into a ball in the sun.

If he was being honest with himself, Gregory was glad that Hannah had the presence of mind to leave him the dragon—even though Sal still kind of freaked him out.

Gregory was getting better at trusting people, and machines had always held his confidence, but there was something about a lizard turned into a mythical beast that still didn't fit right with his sense of reason. Sure, Sal had been nothing but useful in their battles against Adrien and as they travelled to the ends of Irth. But who knew when some sort of magical miswiring could occur, causing the beast to start eating his way through the crew, starting with Gregory.

He just wished Hannah would have sent back Laurel instead. Even Parker or Karl would have been fine. At least they weren't likely to bite him by accident.

Well, Karl might. But only if he was drinking.

Ducking below deck, he slowed to a pause by Ezekiel's aft cabin. He listened, but heard nothing. Could the man stay in a mystical trance for the rest of his days? For a moment, Gregory considered checking in on him, but he took Hannah's commands seriously.

Ezekiel was not to be bothered. She said that interrupting his work could scramble his brains, and the last thing they needed was a dragon and a wizard gone astray by magical meltdown.

Once in the pilot's seat, Gregory took a moment to scan the landscape below. The window looking out of the bow of the boat provided the best perspective on what was happening on the ground.

Just barely making out the village that dotted the edge of the sea, he saw nothing else that seemed like a threat. Squinting toward the woods on the ridgeline, he wondered where Laurel could be. He smiled, imagining her return to the ship. In this story, he scooped her up into his arms, said something charming, and landed a kiss on her full lips.

Pull it together, Gregory thought as he grabbed the stick and eased the *Unlawful* toward the open field on the top of the hill. It followed his command easily and settled on the ground with only a minor bump.

He grabbed a wrench to tighten down any loose nuts and headed for the hangar hatch. It took a while to open, but he didn't trust himself climbing down the ropes. He grabbed the crank and started spinning. The door groaned and banged as it lowered to the ground.

As far as he could tell, it was the only design flaw on the whole ship. That and the mysterious dial in the control room.

As the the door opened, he was greeted by Sal who was panting and waiting for him on the grass.

"Can you just stay on the ship? Please. I'm trying to make repairs. No offense, but your middle name is Destruction."

Sal frowned as best he could, then stepped back on the ship.

As his boots hit the dirt, Gregory sighed. All the others made it a priority to get off the ship, to connect with the land beneath him. Gregory hadn't understood that urge. He never was one for long walks through the woods. But as he looked around and smelled the fresh air, he had to admit that it made him feel slightly more human.

Walking the length of the ship, Gregory stopped and tested a few nuts here and there. A massive hail storm hit several days back, which gave the ship quite a beating. If it wasn't for the fact that Karl was puking his guts out, the rearick would have tried to throw Gregory overboard. He blamed Gregory every time the *Unlawful* hit the slightest breeze.

As he neared the front, Gregory noticed a small corner of the ship's hull was bent outward. The added drag was probably what was throwing his steering out of whack. It was a simple fix, and Gregory ran back inside to grab a bag full of random tools. Half an hour's worth of work and he had torched, bent, and banged the piece back into place.

One last lap around the *Unlawful* and everything seemed in place. He smiled, thinking about his father. Naturally, their relationship didn't end well, with the whole sacrifice his son to Adrien's war-machine thing, but in all of his time caring for the ship, Gregory couldn't help to admire his father's tedious work and careful construction.

He imagined him walking the length of the ship as it sat in the factory, testing the torque on each and every one of the bolts before giving it the OK to be flown. He was a master at his craft —if only he had been able to see that what a thing does is as important as how it's built.

He turned the corner, eyes on the hull, when the sound of heavy breathing and grunting pulled his eyes from his father's masterpiece. He looked, assuming he would find Sal playing nearby. Instead he saw two figures making their way up the hill.

Gregory's blood ran cold.

It was immediately clear they were remnant, with their dull red eyes, sallow skin, and ragged clothes. He had never seen one in person before, but knew their minds were bent on only one thing—the kill. They approached cautiously, staring at the monstrous machine sitting in the otherwise natural setting.

"Shit," Gregory said under his breath as he ducked back behind the other side of the ship, out of sight of the killers.

They were coming fast, and he could hear their nearly inhuman communication as they came his way.

"What the 'ell is 'at?"

"Dunno. But it's man work, that's for sure. I bet there's food inside."

Gregory looked around for escape, but the rope ladder was a way off, and he wasn't sure if he could make it before they rounded the corner. He hit the dirt and rolled into a small stand of bushes nearby. Holding his breath, he prayed silently to the Matriarch that they'd continue on without spotting him in the weeds.

One of the remnant ran his hand along the boat's hull, grinning the whole time. The other paused and sniffed into the open air. His head pivoted toward Gregory. Yanking on the arm of the other remnant, he pointed toward the spot where Gregory lay, shaking in the dirt.

"Save me, Matriarch," he whispered.

The two slunk toward him, taking their time. Eyes darting around the area, Gregory realized that the remnant were more equipped than most gave them credit for. They weren't mindless beasts, but they still lacked the part of a human that gave them an inkling of empathy for any living thing. Begging for mercy would accomplish shit.

Gregory gripped his wrench tightly, knowing it was the only weapon he had. For a moment, he considered magic, but if he wasn't able to conjure a fireball in the safety of the classroom, what good would it do him here when his life was in danger?

The two remnant stood almost directly over him, when a loud *woosh* shattered the natural silence around him.

Looking up, the remnant saw something more unbelievable than the airship. A mighty lizard with a scaled back and wings swooped down low and nearly took their heads off. They grunted as they pointed and shouted at the thing.

Gregory, realizing that Sal had given him his chance, leaped from the bushes. With a shout manlier than anything he'd ever done before, he crashed into the smaller of the two and brought him to the ground. With three swift blows, he crushed the head of the remnant, its body lying motionless beneath him.

Thank you, he thought to both the Matriarch and the dragon.

But his gratefulness melted into terror as the other one turned to attack. He pulled a sword, rusty and jagged and as wild as the remnant itself. Gregory imagined how it would feel slicing through his stomach.

Pausing, the remnant laughed at the sight of the puny man sitting over his fallen comrade. The teeth that actually remained in its mouth were yellow and pointed.

Arcing the sword high over his head, the remnant stepped toward Gregory, and brought down the sword with the power of three men. Instinctually, Gregory raised the metal wrench in defense. With a clash of metal on metal, the tool saved his scalp, but the blow was enough to send the wrench out of his hand, tumbling in the dirt out of reach.

Gregory raised his hands and forced a smile. "Maybe we can make a deal. What is it that you want?"

The remnant laughed again. "Dinner."

He dropped a solid fist into Gregory's face. He felt like a mouse being toyed with by a tomcat.

The remnant pulled back the sword with both hands, ready to carve off a hefty meal for himself.

Out of nowhere, Sal descended in between them, dropping the remnant backwards on his ass and sending dirt and sod into the air. The dragon lifted his chin and let out a howl that would stop the bravest warrior in her tracks.

Before the remnant had a chance to attack—or run for his life —Sal pounced.

Gregory wanted to look away, but he couldn't.

Sal's head, with open jaws, shot forward, ripping the throat of the remnant wide open. Then he batted it's lifeless head back and forth with his talons, making sure the dead would stay just as he was. When the remnant didn't move, Sal stepped back, looking almost confused.

"Sal," Gregory shouted. But the dragon only stared at the dead. He shouted again. "Sal, it's OK. It's over. You saved me, just like Hannah knew you would."

At the sound of her name, the dragon's head snapped toward him, eyes smiling.

"We're safe now."

Sal walked over to Gregory, who took some time to run his nails over the dragon's hide.

"Thank you," he whispered. "But do me a favor. Don't tell Hannah that I almost pissed myself."

Sal nudged Gregory's hip with his snout, and then snapped in the opposite direction, standing up in attention.

"What is it…"

The answer to his question was climbing the hill toward him.

Gregory cursed as he watched a dozen or more remnant running in their direction.

CHAPTER TEN

The sun was getting lower in the sky behind them as the group continued their march toward Kofken. Silent with the single-mindedness of soldiers, Dardanus and his men led the way, while Laurel could be seen skipping around the trees. Hannah dropped back and walked alongside Aysa.

"You've got balls, girl," she said, falling into step with her.

"What? No, I don't. Do women where you come from?" She glanced down at Hannah's crotch. "Huh?"

Hannah laughed. She liked the kid more and more. "Nah. We have them removed from birth. They only make you stupid and lusty."

"Maybe I should look into it. I'm pretty good at losing body parts." She waved the stub where her arm once was in Hannah's direction.

Walking in silence for a minute, Hannah finally asked. "What the hell happened there?"

"This?" Aysa raised her elbow again. "Well, a few years ago, Dardanus up there just kept talking shit. I don't even remember what it was about. But I challenged him to a fight. Told him that if I won, he'd have to spend the rest of his life wearing nothing but a skirt. If he won, he could take my arm. He's a pretty trust-worthy guy, so when he won, he took his prize."

Hannah stared at her, unblinking.

"You're shitting me."

Aysa stopped. Her face lacked all expression. She shook her head. "Yeah. I'm shitting you," she said with a laugh.

"I hate you and love you all at once," Hannah replied joining the laughter. "Sorry, I shouldn't have asked. You don't need to tell me."

The two walked in silence for a while, Aysa's joke unable to break the tension. Finally, she said, "It's fine. It's my life—I learned to not feel embarrassed by it a long time ago. When I was young, only eight years old, roamers struck Baseek, and struck us hard. There were always times we didn't feel safe, but the throwers stationed on the cliff walls were generally enough to hold back attacks. But that day, they came in force, with numbers like we'd never seen before or since.

"They came in by night without lights. Taking out our throwers before they could raise the alarm. Then they rushed us all at once, setting fires to homes and killing everything that stood in their way. But they didn't just come to kill, they came to take. Women, children—anyone weak enough not to resist."

"And they took you?" Hannah asked.

The girl nodded.

"I was chained together with dozens of other Baseeki—as well as folks from all the places they had hit prior to Baseek. Two days into my captivity, I learned what they intended to do with us. Apparently, they march their prisoners for thousands of miles, then sell whoever survives the journey into work camps—so far away from their homes, that even if they did escape, they'd never be able to return.

"Once I learned that, I knew I had to escape—no matter the cost. So, I stole a knife from a particularly stupid guard, and that night, I did what had to be done. I made my escape. But freedom has its cost."

"Holy shit," Hannah said, wondering if she would have the strength that this girl had.

"I was lucky compared to the poor bastards who wouldn't come with me. I healed, moved on. Their lives are gonna be hell. In all fairness, I've got it pretty good. I even managed to pay a few of the roamers back on my way out of camp. My only regret is that I didn't kill more of them."

Hannah nodded, while making a mental note. If they had time, she and the *Unlawful* would try and visit one of these work camps, and let them know just what she thought about their operation.

"Well you seem to get around OK. I saw you fly down that cliff face. And you've got some wicked good aim, too. But I bet that makes life pretty hard."

Aysa nodded. "Sure. But whose life isn't hard? I had always been an orphan, but once I made it back home, the Baseeki took good care of me. They really are a loyal people. But most of them don't know what to do with me. I think my missing arm makes them feel awkward. So, I spend most of my time in the hills, away from the village. That's how I got to be so damn good at climbing and fighting."

Aysa grew quiet again, glancing over at Hannah a few times for approval to go on, and a sign that she could trust her. Getting neither, she continued anyway. "Everyone in Baseek treats me either like a freak or a liability. Everyone except for Sam. He's always been nice to me. If it weren't for him, I imagine I would have just walked off one night... But if a person can feel love from just one other, maybe that's enough. Not that I'd call what he feels for me love or anything. He's just not a dick. It's nice."

"It is," Hannah said, thinking of Will and how the two of them got through their mother's death and father's treachery. "One good person can make up for a thousand douche nuggets, at least that's what I've figured out. And I think you're pretty special, regardless of how he feels for you."

"Either way, I'll probably never know for sure. Not now."

"Don't worry," Hannah said. "We'll get Samet back."

"I know. It's just that—"

Aysa's words were cut short as she saw Dardanus stopped in the path ahead, his hand up indicating they should be still and silent. He turned and crouched, motioning to the others to do the same. Hannah and Aysa crept low up the path to see what was going on.

"Damn, roamers, I think," Dardanus said. "Looks like a pretty good-sized group, too."

Hannah could feel Aysa tense up beside her. She pushed past him and took a look—Hannah followed suit. Dardanus had won her approval, so far, as a decent human being, but she insisted on assessing the situation herself.

A group of men and women, all of them burley and dressed in animal hides, sat in a large clearing. Shrill laughter came up from one, as another told a story loudly enough that Hannah could almost hear the details. They obviously weren't concerned with their own safety, and she could only presume they had earned the right to be arrogant from a solid track record in battle.

They were outnumbered by two to one, as far as she could see, and if these nomads were half as badass as Dardanus made them out to be, they'd be trouble to take head on.

Although she'd never met Samet, she searched for him among the roamers. He wasn't there, at least not where she could see him. They could have him bound and out of sight, but she couldn't be sure from where she was crouched in the undergrowth.

"They're off their guard," Dardanus said. "If we run in now, we can drop a few before they know what hit them."

Hannah scrunched her nose. "Very subtle, D. Is that how you approach the ladies, too?"

He cocked his head and shrugged. Hannah realized there probably wasn't much of a dating scene in Baseek. She'd need to clarify. "If we go in hard and fast, you're right, we'll drop a couple, but we're still outnumbered. Would be good to do this with no casualties on team Baseek. Agreed?"

All of the men looked at each other, as if counting off who would live and who would die.

"Sure," Dardanus finally said. "So, what do you suggest?"

"A strategy."

"Ah! By the Matriarch, am I ever glad to run into you guys," Hannah called out, skipping down the path toward the group of roamers laughing by the trail.

Before she could take another step, nearly a dozen bows were drawn, arrows nocked and ready for action. They were fast.

Really fast.

Dardanus had overestimated the kind of drop they would have had on the group if they had rushed in. It would have been a bloodbath. Not to mention, there were more than she could see from their vantage point. A quick estimation put their number at eighteen, maybe twenty. Almost twice the number of Baseeki.

Stumbling back, with feigned fear on her face, Hannah threw her hands into the air. "Whoa, whoa, whoa! Easy there, friends. I don't mean any harm. I'm unarmed. Just a girl on an adventure, that's all."

The biggest and ugliest of the bunch lowered his bow and stepped toward her, muscles bulging beneath his tight leather clothes. "Out in the wild without a weapon? I'd call you an idiot with a deathwish."

"If an idiot is someone who loves the feeling of wind in her hair and the smell of salt water, then I'm guilty as charged." She tossed her hair with her hand and giggled. "But I do need some help. I'm looking for a city where I'm to meet my friends." She scrunched her nose. "I think it is called Penile, it's in the lower region."

One of the other men dropped his bow. "Darling, I know all about Penile in the lower region. Just come with me, and I'll give you a tour. But a warning, once you see the tower, you'll never want to leave."

He laughed and the others joined him.

Hannah forced a chuckle at his joke. "I heard that your penile is quite withered with lack of use."

"*Ohhh!*" the crowd shouted.

The man raised his bow, leveling an arrow at her head, but the leader of the group waved him down. "You've been traveling, have you?"

Hannah nodded, doing anything she could to keep the conversation rolling. She knew her team needed time to get ready, and if they were lucky, Hannah could get the information she needed without resorting to violence.

"Then maybe you know what the hell that thing is?"

Hannah watched as all of the Marauders leaned in. For the life of her, she had no idea what they were talking about. "What thing?"

A woman, nearly as tall and as broad as the men, stood. "Enough. Let's tie the wench up and put her over the fire. That'll make her talk... or at least squeal like a pig."

Grunts of agreement surrounded Hannah as three of them approached, arms outstretched. She glanced over at the fire and realized this wasn't a scare tactic. She would soon be their pig on a spit.

Fear built in her gut and ran through every ounce of her flesh. She could feel the power in her blood running wild beneath her skin.

Shit. So much for the diplomatic approach. *Anytime now, guys,* she thought, looking past the raving group and toward the woods.

Three men threw wood on the fire, laughing to themselves. Another pulled back on his bow, shouting, "Let me get the pig ready."

He let loose the arrow.

Everything slowed. She could see the shaft and its trajectory for her. Swiping her hand across her body, she raised a shield. The arrow grazed off of it and into the woods.

The marauders' jaws went slack. A young woman, nearly Hannah's age pointed and yelled, "She's a damned witch. Get her!"

The remaining crowd rushed her, and that was apparently what the Baseeki were waiting for. Before the roamers could cut the space between her and them in half, a volley of rocks came flying out of the woods. Each one found their targets—crushing bone and skull. The unlucky roamers dropped to the dirt, a few unconscious, the others cursing and rolling around in pain.

But the roamers had clearly fought Baseeki before. They turned toward the woods, blindly firing arrow after arrow through the trees. More rocks came, but they were fewer and less accurate.

Three more bodies dropped, but Hannah watched as a large woman took a rock to the shoulder and remained standing.

Shit, Hannah thought. *They are badass. This might not work.*

"To cover!" one of the men yelled, and they all scurried to find shelter behind boulders and trees. It would be damned near impossible to root them out with bolas and rocks.

Seeing that the ranged game was a losing battle, the Baseeki decided to try a hand to hand fight.

Just as Hannah had planned it.

Dardanus rushed down the hill from behind the roamers. Laurel, Aysa, and two of his men were with him. They screamed like the world was coming to an end, and they were the ones making it happen.

Distracted by the volley of rocks in front of them, the roamers were unprepared for the assault from the rear.

Bodies clashed against bodies, and a half dozen roamers were down before the rest could drop their bows in favor of short swords for close combat. Hannah watched in awe, realizing that the Baseeki and their bolas were a force to be reckoned with in close proximity. Dardanus dropped three without missing a beat and turned to face more. Laurel was spinning and slashing as always, and Hannah saw Aysa grab a roamer's hand and turn their own sword against them.

"Give 'em hell!" Hannah yelled as she walked toward the fray.

"You're mine, you little bitch," a voice said from behind her.

Hannah spun, drawing up fireballs as she turned. "I hate that word." She launched the quickly made orbs at a large man. He sidestepped one, but the other landed on his chest, knocking him back a step.

He beat the fire out with his hands, then looked down at sizzling leather and laughed. "All you got, honey? It's gonna take more than your damn tricks to take me down."

He pulled his short sword and gritted his teeth.

"All I got? That was just a warm up, *bitch*."

Hannah's eyes turned deep red. She cleared out her mind, and tried to truly connect with the natural world around her. She dropped to the ground, pressing her hands deep into the earth.

"What the hell are you doing?" he said. "Stand and fight me you bit—"

Before he could finish, a vine shot from the woods to their side. Then another, and another. Tendrils from the natural world wrapped him from head to toe. He screamed, more out of shock than pain.

Soon, his screams turned to laughter as he began hacking at

the vines with his sword. "This is your master plan? I ain't afraid of no damn leaves."

Hannah ignored him, and for every vine he severed, two more swirled around him.

He sliced another, still laughing, though his face had begun to turn red. "When I get you—"

"You won't get me, dipshit. I'm Hannah from Arcadia. You're nothing more than an ant beneath my boot."

Her eyes blazed red as she slowly rose to her feet. She twisted her palms, turning them into fists.

"Wait," he said. "What are you doing? Stop!"

She paused for a second, her closed fists held tightly in front of her. She looked upward, like she was thinking through a riddle. Finally, she shrugged. "No. I don't think I will. Now, squeal like a pig."

She pushed her hands forward, palms outward. At once, the vines erupted into bright blue flames.

His screams didn't last for long before the vines dropped his lifeless body to the ground.

CHAPTER ELEVEN

"Who you calling a kid?" Laurel screamed as she lashed her rope at an attacker.

The flint at the end found his jugular. He gripped his throat, uselessly trying to keep his lifeblood inside his body. She spun and another was on her, too close for her rope blade. The woman swung a sloppy right at her, and Laurel pivoted a second too slow. The roundhouse grazed off her chin.

"You skeezy wench," she said, rubbing the spot as she circled around the roamer.

"Gonna teach you how a grown woman fights. Too bad you'll be too dead to use it," the large woman laughed.

"Not sure what 'too dead' means, but bring it."

The woman pulled a sword and lunged, missing to the left, and then lunged again. This time, Laurel stepped to the right and grabbed the woman's arm. She pulled hard, letting the woman's momentum carry her straight into Dardanus who finished her off with a flick of his bola.

"If that's how a grown woman fights, then I'm happy to remain young." Laurel bowed low. "Thank you for the assist, fine Baseeki."

He grinned and gave an awkward bow in return.

"Shit! Look out." Laurel pointed behind him.

Dardanus spun, finding no one there.

"You are so gullible!" Laurel yelled and raced back into battle.

Three of the roamers cut through the melee, their eyes on Laurel.

"Shit, buddy, I can't take them all," she said.

Without another word, Devin shot out of her cloak and hit the ground in a full sprint. Leaping, the squirrel hit the one in the middle in the groin, bending him in half before scurrying up his back, biting and scratching all the way. The man swatted at the fat squirrel, but she was way too fast.

"One down," Laurel laughed. "Guess I have the two of you."

The men looked at each other and grinned. A lifetime on the road had given them the opportunity to put plenty of notches on their belts. A girl with a squirrel wasn't going to best them.

At once, they charged, short swords drawn.

Laurel grabbed a low-hanging limb. Her eyes flashed green, and the tree pulled her ten feet into the air as they passed under. She dropped with a shout, driving her dagger into the back of one of the men.

The other grabbed her by the cloak as she withdrew the knife. "Time to say goodnight, sweetheart," he whispered into her ear.

"Goodnight, sweetheart," Aysa cried as she plowed into him shoulder first.

Instinctually, the man dropped Laurel and spun to face his attacker. "Ah, the one-armed bandit. It's not even fair."

"You're right," Aysa replied. "This will be all too easy. I can tie my good arm behind my back if you think it will help."

His grin disappeared, and he rushed her wildly.

Laurel watched in awe at the girl's skill with her bola. She had seen the Baseeki take down targets from a distance, but up close they were just as deadly. Aysa held one half of the bola in her massive hand, and spun the other side in a criss crossing pattern in front of her.

The roamer lunged with his blade, but Aysa easily used the bola to knock it aside. Before he could respond, she cracked him alongside the jaw, sending him spinning.

Before he could right himself, she planted her huge foot in his chest and knocked him to the ground.

He struggled to stand. "You stupid—" But his insult was cut short as she whipped her bola toward him, smashing in his face with a direct hit.

"Impressive," Laurel said as she watched the girl retrieve her weapon.

"I do all right. But that tree thing? What the hell?"

Laurel shrugged. "It's all about who you know."

Hannah fought off the remaining roamers by the side of a Baseeki warrior. He was good, and she couldn't help but admire his moves.

She was about to compliment him on a particularly awesome throw with his bola when a quiet whistle flew past her. She watched as an arrow suddenly burst through the soft spot in the man's stomach. Another took him in the leg.

"Get down," Hannah screamed, shoving the warrior to the ground.

She waved her hand over him and created a small shield to ward off further attacks. Her eyes turned for the ridgeline. Her plan had worked well: the two-pronged attack kept the roamers off balance and prevented them from using their arrows effectively.

But someone had broken out of the fight and was acting like a sniper, raining down death from above. Arrows whistled around her. A near miss cruised past her ear, and a shrill cry called out behind her. One of Dardanus's men took it in the throat.

Turning her attention back to the ridge, she saw the coward, crouched beside a pile of rocks. She blazed a fireball and launched it in his direction, more to draw his fire than anything. Drawing up her own shield, she sprinted uphill, driving toward the man. He fired arrow after arrow, each one deflecting or shattering against her magical shield.

The man's eyes widened when she was a yard off. He dropped his bow and reached for his blade, but he was too late.

Hannah pulled her dagger from her belt. Driving her blade into his gut, she pulled the steel up toward the man's heart. His mouth dropped open, as if he wanted to say some last words, but there was nothing.

She released his body, and wiped the knife on the fallen man's leathers. "Thanks, Karl," she said as she sheathed the dagger, before dropping to the ground nearly exhausted.

Hannah sat on the hill, watching the rest of the fight. She wanted to help, but there was no energy left in her legs. And besides, team Baseek had the fight locked down. She watched as a young, one-armed girl dropped the last warrior with a solid punch to the jaw.

She exhaled and let her head fall between her legs for a moment, thanking the Matriach and the Patriarch for a swift victory before dragging herself to her feet and descending the hill.

She could hear her new friends cheering as they stood victorious over the vanquished.

Bodies were strewn around the marauders camp. Nearly all of them the enemy. Hannah surveyed the situation and found that they had lost a third of their own forces in the battle. It was a lot, but far less than if they had run out bolas blazing.

One man, the guard she had covered with her shield, leaned against a rock, clutching the arrow in his gut. He paid little attention to the one in his leg. Dardanus crouched over him, holding the man's hand.

"We'll lose him," he said, as Hannah approached.

"Like hell we will." She passed the giant guard a grin. "We've got this. Pull the arrows out."

She waved Laurel over as the man screamed in agony.

"How's your energy?" Hannah asked the druid.

"Been better. Way better. And healing isn't—"

Hannah held her hand up. "It's going to need to be tonight. You've got the leg, I'll get the um," she glanced down at the wound on the man's stomach, knowing the arrow pierced organs, "more complicated matters."

They both focused what little energy they had left, and the man's wounds began to heal over. Color returned to his face.

"What the hell?" Aysa whispered from behind them.

"Thank you," he wheezed as he passed into unconsciousness. The hole in his stomach had closed, but Hannah knew he was far from truly healed. He would probably feel pain from that wound for the rest of his life.

Dardanus put a hand on Hannah's shoulder and nodded his thanks.

"Still think we're out to get you guys?" she asked, raising her brows.

He laughed. "If so, it's strategy that goes way over my head."

She eyed his tall frame. "I get the feeling that very little goes over your head."

Before he could answer, a voice rang out. "I've got a live one over here!"

———

The world spun as Karl walked through the town. His more than gentle buzz had him wondering just how much he had to drink in the cell. He tried to do the math, but quit after he almost tripped on a stray rock. It didn't much matter anyway. With Hannah out looking for the chief's son, he was sure he'd be treated like a king, even if the king needed to be locked behind metal bars from time to time.

Karl had no problem with the girls playing hero—but if the chief wanted Karl to play the respectful diplomat, he chose the wrong rearick.

Come to think of it, most rearick made for piss poor diplomats.

The sun was setting as the guards led him down the road—if you could call it that. The route they took was more of a foot-path, created by the habitual patterns of a simple people who thrived on the simple life.

In many ways, Baseek reminded him of the Heights. They were a people in a place who knew who they were and what they were about. Small town living bred loyalty—and a fierce desire to protect the homeland. Karl understood this—but he had also seen enough of the world to know that small communities devel-oped their own blind spots.

It was that naïveté that Karl hoped to work to his advantage if the need arose.

Ducking through tight passages, they finally arrived at a small hut near the edge of the village. It was a simple building—certainly not the chief's quarters—and Karl noticed it was the building situated furthest from the rest.

Odd choice for a meeting of the minds, Karl thought, sobering up slightly as they stepped inside.

The guards moved him through the doors with enough hospi-tality to show they meant no harm, and then set him on a chair in the middle of the room. One of the guards took lengths of rope and tied Karl's arms down tight behind him.

"Hey? We really need this, lads?" he protested as they did their job in silence. "Scheisse, how am I supposed to drink like this?"

Ignoring him, the men left the hut, and Karl sat alone in

silence, wishing he were back behind the bars with his friends, sipping on the ale. Although he wouldn't say it to the man's face, Parker was right. Something was very off. Within minutes, he had gone from living the sweet life under house arrest to being fastened to a chair in a hut that just happened to be out of earshot from any living being.

There wasn't much time to dream of better times, because the door swung open. Karl watched as the woman, Vatan, entered the room, flanked by two guards. She was nearly as tall as them, with the strange proportions unique to the Baseeki

"You ain't the chief," Karl said.

She took two long steps toward him, hips swaying almost seductively—like a reed blowing in the wind. The men closed the door behind them, one standing on each side.

"Oh, poor Sef. He doesn't have the stomach for the work that I do. Guess that's why he keeps me around. Now, rearick, tell me who you really are—you and your friends—and we can just put you back in your little room with a bucket full of brew." She smiled and waited for a response.

"There ain't no more to tell, lass. Ya got it from Hannah last night, no need for me ta get into it again."

Vatan took another step so she was standing nearly between his legs spread and tied to the chair. "You almost look like you're telling the truth. Funny how one can become so good at lying, if they practice enough." She reached her large hand toward him and ran a finger down his forehead. She followed the bridge of his nose to the tip before pulling it back and landing a fierce open palmed smack across his face. "Now, enough bullshit. Time to talk. I want to know who all of you are and how you acquired such fascinating powers."

So much for vacation, he thought.

He grit his teeth and stared her in the eye. "You do know how to sweet talk a guy. Why don't you unbind me? I'd be happy to show ya my powers."

Taking a step back, Vatan wound up and landed a hook to Karl's stomach. The blow rocked him, and for a moment he wondered if he would lose some of the ale in his stomach.

He sat up tall, a drunken smile on his face. "Is that it? You Baseeki may have large hands, but you've got limp wrists. It's like takin' a punch from a six-year-old. I tell ya what, why don't we skip the 'tell me everything' bit and ya just let me outta here. Otherwise, this is gonna take all night. I ain't the kind that cracks easy."

"We'll see," Vatan said. Turning, she said to one of the guards, "You stay and work him over. Do whatever you need to make him break. We need more information, and we're damn sure not going to get it by treating them like kings."

The man approached, rubbing his hands together, a psychopath's grin on his face.

Vatan moved for the door, the other guard followed. Looking over her shoulder, she said, "Oh, and Drake..."

"Ma'am?"

"Keep it below the neck. Not sure we want the honored guests walking around with signs of our little talk. It would only raise more questions."

He affirmed her command and was slugging away with his long arms and massive fists at Karl's midsection before the door was even closed. A sweat broke on the Baseeki's brow, and he panted heavily. Stepping back, he asked, "Ready yet, you mountain prick?"

Karl breathed deeply and felt at least three of his ribs crunching on his left side. "It's like I said, you ocean twats got limp wrists. When are we gonna get to the real fun? Ya punch like a child, and I imagine you got the mind of one, too. What's yer play here?"

"Information. She needs it, I get it—from anyone."

Shrugging the best he could while tied to the chair, Karl said, "Well, ya better get back to work then, cause I ain't even close."

Drake, the guard did just that. His eyes grew wild as he pounded on Karl's chest and gut. Suddenly, he stopped. "Did you say something?" he gasped.

"Don't think so. I may have been whistlin' to myself. This whole thing's a little borin'."

The man glanced around the room, then raised a fist to go back to work. Two slugs and he stopped, looking around the room confused. "I swear I heard..."

He trailed off, turned, and left the hut, hunting for the source of the voices. Karl took the chance to visibly wince from the pain the man's powerful upper body delivered. He'd refuse to show it to him though.

As Karl tried to gather himself, an image of Hadley appeared in front of him.

"Scheisse, man, that's a good trick. You could have maybe started a little earlier, though."

The hologram of his friend winked and then blinked back out of existence right before Drake returned.

"Must have been some damned kids." He crossed the room again and stood over Karl. "Let's be reasonable, shall we? Just give me some information about your friends and their powers. And that damned flying beast your girl brought with her. And I can get ya back to your drink."

"I already told ya kid, there's no big secret to uncover. My friends and I are just wandering do-gooders, trying to help. In fact, I bet they're on their way back now with your Samet."

Now that Karl knew Hadley was in the game, everything had changed. The mystics could get inside almost anyone's head, chat them up. The most powerful could even place bits of information in the mind of another unguarded from their wiles. Although they were a long way from the cell, he thought maybe this was what Hadley was up to.

Drake raised his hand, then stopped and looked around the room again.

"Probably yer conscience dickin' with ya," Karl said to the bewildered man.

"My what?"

"Ya know, like the better parts of ya sayin' this ain't right. That I've done nothin' to deserve this," Karl did his best to grin. "I always listen to mine. Kept me out of a world of shit a time or two before."

The man stood and looked at the wall, as if he were listening. "There it goes again. A voice, but I can't quite make it out."

Karl couldn't be certain, but he was pretty damned sure that Hadley was upstairs, dancing around in the kid's mind, probably laying a suggestion or two along the way. He decided to play along.

"Aye, that's definitely the conscience. I know it all too well. Listen, pal... let's just think this through. What did I ever do to ya?"

"Huh?"

Karl laughed. "I mean, you're here beatin' the livin' shit outta me, and I'd say there's a bit of ya in the back of yer mind sayin', 'Drake, this makes no bloody sense.' Am I right?"

"But Vatan said—"

"Who cares what Vatan said, or the chief said, or even what I'm sayin'? What does the inner Drake say? Do you wanna be doin' this?"

"Damn. I guess... I guess I never really thought about it."

"Aye," Karl spouted. "We don't so much when we're young, like ya are now. I did some bad things too when I was yer age. It still haunts me at night—probably why I drink so much. Cause over time, ya learn to listen to the better angels. And it's better if they're happy with how ya lived."

The man slowly nodded. "You think what I'm doing's bad?"

"Well, it sure as shit ain't saintly. But I'll make a deal with ya. Ya take me back the cell, and we'll call it even. No hard feelings.

What do ya say?" Karl's eyes looked down at the vines and then back at the guard.

"Hey, you're not trying to pull one over one me, are you?"

Karl smiled as warmly as he could. "Come on. Rearick's honor. I know ya don't know my people from the fish in yer sea, but one thing a rearick never does is lie," Karl lied.

"Guess this all makes sense," the man said as he drew his dagger and cut Karl free. "But you might need to help me explain it to Vatan."

"Oh, sure, kid. Nothing to it. A woman smart as her... She'll totally understand."

CHAPTER TWELVE

"I'll never talk ya witch; just finish it *now!*" the wounded roamer screamed into Hannah's face.

He was propped against a tree with Laurel's vines holding him place. His face was seriously swollen from where a bola or a stray rock hit him in the face, but Hannah didn't imagine he was very pretty to look at before.

Dardanus's men wanted to string him up the moment the fighting stopped, but Hannah convinced them to let her try talking first. They needed the intel, and she was hoping that he would be more likely to share it with her.

"Oh, don't worry, we'll get to that last part... If you don't cooperate. But let's get serious, shall we?"

His eyes narrowed at the calm demeanor of the foreign woman who knelt over him.

"We already know how this will end. You refuse. We torture. You refuse... blah, blah, blah. Finally, you tell us exactly what we're looking for. Let's skip the blah, blah, blah."

The man said nothing. Instead, he spat his dirty saliva on Hannah's face. She wiped it with the back of her hand. "OK. First time I've actually had someone have the balls to do that to me."

She landed a fist to the bruised side of his head and felt it go a little squishy. He grunted in pain.

"Geez, man, you gotta get that looked at. One last chance, and then I bring on the blah, blah, blahs."

"Screw you, witch. What are you gonna do to me?"

"Me?" Hannah grinned. "Nothing. You're not really worth my time. But my friend Devin is hungry."

"Devin?" his eyes grew with confusion. "Who's he?"

"Ah shit, you've already made another mistake. Devin's a *she*, and *she's* terribly cute—until she starts chewing on your face."

Hannah made a clicking sound with her tongue, and the squirrel crawled out of Laurel's sleeve and ran over to Hannah's side.

"All right, Devin. Do your thing."

The squirrel crawled up his chest and the man tried to scurry away.

"Laurel, a little help here?"

"My pleasure," the druid said. Her eyes turned green, and the weeds around the man grew thicker, enveloping his wrists and ankles, holding him to the tree.

"What... what the hell is this? You're a bunch of freaks!" he shouted.

"Yeah. We are freaks. And Devin is freakishly hungry. So, it's time for you to talk. What do you know about Samet?"

"Bite me."

"You heard him, Devin." She looked down into the squirrel's black eyes. "Left cheek. If you will."

Devin jumped, landing on the man's face. He screamed as the squirrel's claws groped, trying to find purchase. Finally digging in, Devin bit down on his cheek and then again.

"Shit!" the man screamed.

"Yeah, I know," Hannah crooned. "It's pretty bad, right? Listen, I've heard some pretty bad things about you roamers. And you weren't exactly nice to me when I came into your camp. I mean, you were actually going to roast me over the fire. Sure, I was only pretending to be lost. All a part of my master trap—but you didn't know that."

Hannah spotted a particularly dirty spot on her cloak and dusted it off nonchalantly as she continued with a sarcastic smile. "So, I shouldn't feel too bad about putting you through all this pain. But I'm feeling generous today. Chock it up to my girlish nature. All your homies are dead around you. You're the last one left. I get all that honor stuff, but come on, we all know you'd sell your own mother if it got you what you wanted. Nobody's going to know. Tell me about Samet."

"Please," he cried. "Just end me."

Hannah sighed. "What's your name?"

He paused for a second, searching her words for some trap. Finally, he said, "Altan."

"Al, listen, we're the good guys here. You're the bad guy. We don't want to kill you, we just want to know where our friend is. Now, tell me about Samet."

The man stared up at her indignantly. He was a man of twisted principle, but it was becoming clear that even perverted principle was not easily shaken.

"OK," Hannah said. "Time for the game changer."

Reaching down, she began to loosen the belt around his waist.

"Sorry to do this to you, Dev, but I need you to go south on Al here."

"OK, I think we're crossing a line here—" Hannah could hear Dardanus behind her. Laurel placed her hand on his shoulder. "She knows what she's doing. Where we come from, it's an effective interrogation tool."

"You... you wouldn't," the man said with a whimper.

"YOU WERE GOING TO COOK ME OVER THE FIRE!" she yelled. "Do I look like the kind of person who would bluff about this?"

"I... I..."

"Devin, chop chop. We don't have all day."

The squirrel blinked twice and then scurried down the man's abdomen.

"Shit. No! I'll talk. I'll talk."

Hannah smiled. "There we are, Al, all of us reasonable, human beings. I guess the way to a man's heart is through his—" she glanced down at him "—twig and berries. Now, tell me about Samet."

Al's breathing increased, chest heaving up and down. "I don't know any Samet, I swear. Never heard his name before."

Hannah's eyes flashed red as she entered his mind, checking to see if he was being honest. "Good start, Al. I know because there was one thing you were right about. I am a witch, and I can tell when you are lying. So, don't pull any shit, or Dev here will be dining on your bolas, understand."

Altan nodded.

"OK, next question. If you weren't up here because of Samet, what brought you and the others up to this hill?"

His eyes moved from Hannah to the beast on his torso and back. "We were sent here to investigate the thing."

"What thing?"

He stared at her, his eye twitching.

"Tell me what thing," Hannah said, "or Devin will go to town on your *thing*."

"It's crazy, but…" He paused, collecting his words. "The thing in the sky. We've been watching it, like it's from the Gods or something. We were to come, find out what it was, and bring it back to our home. That's all." The man started to weep. "That's all. You just came and got in our damned way. Kent thought you might know something about it. You might be able to tell us."

Hannah leaned in close to the man's face. She could feel his breathing on her cheek. "I do, Al. I do know about it. That thing, the thing in the air brought me here. It brought me to you. And you know what?"

"What?" he whimpered.

"I think it brought me to put an end to all the shit you and your people are doing to the folks who live around here. If you think this is bad, just wait until I'm back aboard my ship. I can visit your home and wipe it off the map." She leaned in closer. "Give me a reason not to. Why should I let ass maggots like you live?"

"Wait... wait, OK. I remember now. We saw some of the long-armed bastards the other day. They were wandering through the hills."

Hannah looked up at Dardanus. His expression somehow even more sober than ever. "Were they OK?"

Al looked confused. "OK?"

"Were they injured or held captive?" Dardanus asked. He leaned down close to the man.

"I don't know. They looked fine to me."

"Was there a boy with them?" Hannah asked, pointing to Aysa. "About her age."

"A boy? No. I don't know. We gave them a pretty wide berth. We were only after the thing in the sky."

"Where did you see them?"

Al described the location to Dardannus, who nodded knowingly. Hannah motioned to Laurel. "Release him. We've got what we need."

The druid's eyes flashed green again, and the weeds retreated. As quickly as they did, Altan took off into the woods—with the speed of a desperate man.

"This is a mistake!" Cal shouted. "We should kill him now."

"I won't kill a man in cold blood," she said. "He gave us what we need. Let's just get on with it."

Cal shook his head. "Letting him go, it will mean trouble later. Mark my words." He pointed a meaty finger in her face. "And that will be on you."

Hannah pushed his hand aside, and stepped right up to him,

face to face. "If trouble comes, then I will rip out its guts and wear them as a dress. Got it? Now, are you going to give me trouble?"

The big man seethed, but then backed away. He had seen what she could do, and he wasn't a fool.

Hannah turned and looked at the other Baseeki. They were all staring at her, awed by her power and her resolve. Even Dardanus had a smile on his face, impressed with the girl.

"Drag the bodies over there." She pointed to a place well beyond the camp. "And bury your dead. We camp here for the night. Tomorrow, we find your prince."

Without a word, the men did exactly as she said.

Parker continued to pace the cell, ten steps in each direction. He'd wear a hole in the floorboards if Karl was gone much longer. In his mind, he ran through the scenarios of what exactly the meeting meant, and what was taking so long. He also, in the depths of his heart, hoped he wouldn't be next.

He had already been tortured once, and it wasn't an experience he was hoping to revisit any time soon.

Sitting on his bunk, perfectly reposed, Hadley mumbled silently with his eyes closed.

"The hell are they doing with him, anyway?" he asked the mystic.

Hadley kept his eyes closed. "Torturing him," he said casually.

"What? How do you know that?" Parker asked, but Hadley kept quiet.

Parker stared for a second, then kept talking to himself. "That settles it then. We need to get out of here."

He stopped pacing long enough to give the bars a shake, drawing a little attention from the porter in the corner of the room. Lowering his voice, he whispered, "We need to break out. Go save Karl and get the hell out of this crazy little town."

Hadley kept up his trance as if he were the only human remaining on the face of Irth.

"Damn it! Stop that. How can you take this all so casually? You need to do something."

Hadley slowly cracked his eyes open. They were covered over in white, which still freaked Parker out a little. "I wasn't doing nothing," he muttered in a monotone. "In fact, I was doing more with my eyes closed than you've done in days."

Parker furrowed his brow, assuming that the mystic was using his gifts, but it still made no sense. He was about to say so, when their door opened. To Parker's disbelief, Karl walked through with one of the guards who had hauled him away. They were talking and laughing like they were the oldest friends in the world.

Parker turned to look at Hadley, but the mystic was grinning from ear to ear. "That's what I was doing." He nodded toward the two men just as Karl landed a hard pat on the guard's back.

"All right, then, Drake. Say hello to your good mother for me. And keep yer head down, OK? Stay away from Vatan until I get the chance to clear all this up."

The guard nodded like a fool. "You got it." He paused, his face tightening in a serious expression. "And, Karl, I can't thank you enough. This conscience thing is really going to change things for me."

"Aye, kid. It did for me. Yer a good fella. Don't let them tell you otherwise." He gave him another slam to the back and shoved him toward the door.

Karl turned back to his cellmates, holding his ribs and wincing when they were finally alone. "Damn, fool has a hell of a hook, I'll tell ya that much."

"And now," Hadley said, "a clear conscience, thanks to us."

The two laughed, and Parker looked more confused than ever. "Spill it. What the hell happened?"

Karl lowered himself onto his cot and held out his empty mug between the bars for the porter to fill it. "Let's just say I take back all the nasty things I ever said 'bout them mindnuts livin' in the clouds. Hadley here did a little mystical tinkerin' inside that boy's noggin'. Certainly saved me little hairy arse."

Karl filled in Parker on the details from his end, allowing Hadley to drop in commentary whenever he wanted.

"Once I was done connecting that douche with his inner voice, I got him talkin' a bit about some other things, too." He took a long slug from the mug, allowing the tension to build. "Seems nothin' is quite what it seems around here."

"How so?" Parker asked.

"Fer starters, let's just say that Vatan and Sef don't precisely see eye to eye on all matters. In fact, that lass convinced my man not to tell the chief 'bout our little conversation in their torture shack."

Parker nodded. "Remember the two of them at the meeting? He was supposed to talk with us, but she seemed to be the one wearing the britches."

"Aye, and who had the biggest balls."

Parker turned to Hadley, who was taking in his friends' glee. "Well, now that you're feeling better, can you take a look under the hood? See what Vatan is really up to?"

"Maybe, but not unless I can get close to her." Hadley called for his own mug of ale. "There's not too many things I can do from afar. Maybe Julianne could, but not me. All I did from here with Karl's friend is plant a few mild suggestions." He pointed at Karl. "That guy did all the heavy lifting."

"That's why I'm so damn sore?" Karl snorted. "Or wait, was it the asskickin' I got while I waited for yer mind tricks?"

"But," Hadley continued, "if I could get close enough to her, preferably without her knowing, then I can get in and really see what's what."

Karl tilted his glass at Parker. "So, we need to get the mind-pilot outta here. And that one, young Arcadian, is up to you."

Parker smiled. "I think I have some ideas on that front. At midnight, we make our move. But there are other things to be accomplished first."

Karl's bushy brows pulled in over his blue eyes. "Like what?"

"First, you need some rest."

"And second?"

"We're getting piss drunk!" Parker replied with some excitement. The rearick laughed. "Finally, something in my wheelhouse." He raised his mug again. "I'll drink to that."

CHAPTER THIRTEEN

Gregory's jaw dropped as the group of remnant, twenty or so in all, crested the rise below them, charging for the top. He couldn't tell if they were male or female, but it was clear they were all scary as hell.

"Shit bucket!" he yelled, his face turning green. There was no time to hide—the remnant clearly saw him—and it was doubtful he could out run them. He stood, paralyzed, until Sal bit his sleeve and began to tug.

Gregory looked down at the dragon, and he realized that Sal was telling Gregory to climb aboard.

"Oh, you've got to be shitting me." His face turned even greener.

Sal tugged harder, with a sense of urgency in his black, beady eyes.

"OK, OK, just let me get my tools. We need them."

Gregory sprinted for the bow of the ship, Sal right behind him. He bent, grabbing the bag of tools he was using, and took a flying leap onto Sal's back. He landed, but his momentum was too great, and he swung off the slippery scales. He spilled to the ground, along with his tools. Before he could respond, five remnant were on him.

He kicked, punched, and swung his wrench, fighting to save his own ass. It was over, and he knew it, but he thought he just might be able to take a few of the soulless bastards with him. One of the beasts bit down on his shoulder. Swinging wildly, Gregory caught him in the skull with the tool, and the thing rolled off him. With a quick kick, he nailed another one square in the crotch.

The others were too much, and he curled up into a defensive ball and tried to remember the Arcadian last rights.

But he wasn't alone.

Sal's roar shred through the clamor, and his talons ripped the flesh of the remnant, giving Gregory the chance to roll out to safety. He launched to his feet and backed up against the ship as Sal shredded the remaining remnant in the first onslaught. As he did his job, many more caught up with their faster companions.

"Sal!" Gregory screamed. But before the dragon could respond, a group of seven had him surrounded. Glancing over their shoulders, he saw more and more crest the rise. There were scores of them.

It was lost.

Reaching down, he snatched the magitech torch from his tool bag, which he used to loosen rusted bolts. He turned the knob as far as it would go, and then busted out the regulator. The contraption hissed with potential.

Gregory pitched it at their feet in the middle of the circle. He contorted his hands, like Hannah had taught him, and sloppily flung them in the direction of the torch. Miraculously, his eyes turned black, and a small stream of fire shot from his hands. It was puny, and he knew it.

But it did the trick.

When his fire reached the torch, it ignited the tiny magitech core, releasing magical energy in every direction. Three remnant screamed and cursed, running off as the unharnessed power burned their flesh.

"Didn't see that coming," Gregory said, impressed by his own ingenuity.

But his celebration didn't last long. The remaining four advanced.

Gregory did the only thing left he could. He acted.

Raising the wrench, he shouted, "Damned remnant, behold, Gregory the great!" He gripped the wrench tightly, praying it would stop quivering in his hand. "Turn back now, and I will spare your lives. Continue, and I will end your meaningless existence."

The creatures stopped, looked at him and then at one another and laughed their asses off.

"I'm gonna eat him screaming," a particularly nasty looking female shouted.

"I'm gonna wear his head as a hat," another joined in.

"So much for intimidation tactics." Gregory mumbled.

He looked at the death staring him in the face, and wondered what Hannah would do if she were in his shoes.

The thought made him go weak at the knees.

But with no escape, and no sign of help on the horizon, the Hannah plan was the only option he had left. He sighed, raised his wrench high into the air and charged the screaming remnant, his voice crackling across the air:

"Death to douche nuggets!"

The party was a mile closer to Kofken, and Dardanus still hadn't uttered more than ten words. Hannah peppered him with a few questions about the lay of the land and what life was like in Baseek, but he only grunted out one-word answers.

Finally, she raised her voice, "What crawled up your ass and died?"

The giant guard stopped and turned to her. "First, I just buried my cousin back there."

Hannah's face fell. She had seen death—a lot of death lately. A part of her was afraid that she might have become numb to it, and she cursed herself for not being a bit more sensitive. "I'm sorry, man. I didn't know."

Dardanus waved her off and even grinned a little. "It's all right. He knew what our job was when he took it. He was glad to fight for his home. I'm proud of him."

As the head guard grew quiet again, Hannah decided to give him his space. She fell back and into pace with Laurel. The druid was walking with a limp, but her face was as serene as ever.

"You all right?" Hannah asked, pointing at her leg.

"Took a shot in the leg from one of those bastards. When it was all finished, and we had healed that guy—" she pointed at the guard they had saved "—I didn't have much in the tank. Later tonight, I should be able to take care of it."

Hannah nodded. "Let me know if you need help." She walked a few more steps without saying anything until Laurel broke the silence.

"That was pretty badass back there."

"Yeah, right," Hannah said. "Nothing like you and that rope blade of yours. I just know a few tricks."

"Bullshit. That thing you pulled with the flaming vines, that's not normal magic. The way you pick and pull from different styles like that—and on the fly, too—it's one of a kind."

Hannah shrugged. Zeke had told her much the same when they started training, but she didn't know if she believed it. Laurel was way better than her at nature magic. Hadley ran circles around her with the mystical stuff. She was pretty good at physical magic, but nothing compared to what Amelia could do.

"Maybe. But I usually just rely on my physical magic. It's what I'm best at. Other than making Sal, or whatever you want to call it, I've not done much that you or the others couldn't. And those few times when I did show some real power, I don't know, it was like something inside of me took control. Don't get me wrong, I'm glad it happened, but I can't really do stuff like that on command."

"Well, maybe you should start trying. Whatever hell quest the Founder is leading us toward, it would be nice to have something out of this world on our side. It's like we say in the Forest, the caged bird flies the highest once it's been set free."

Hannah laughed. "Do they really say shit like that where you're from or do you just make it up on the fly?"

Laurel smiled. "I'll never tell."

They walked the next couple of miles, each lost in their own thoughts. Finally, Hannah asked, "Do you think something's off about this whole thing? I get this feeling that we're going about this all wrong. Do you feel it, too, or is it just this place?"

"You're not wrong. This place is as normal as a ten-foot rearick," Laurel said, laughing at her own joke.

Hannah joined in. "Or a druid lumberjack."

Laurel's face went flat. "Oh, you had to go there, did you? As normal as a Boulevard skank… Oh, wait, that is normal."

"Screw you," Hannah laughed. "So, what do you think is going on? I mean, why haven't we found the bodies of the other guards? That roamer didn't seem to think anything was out of the ordinary when he saw them. I guess he could have been lying."

"No way. You and Devin were pretty persuasive."

"So?"

"Honestly," Laurel sighed. "I think the kid is a damned brat, like some of the noble kids you told me about from the Academy. He probably just wanted attention, so he ran off or something."

"And his guard?"

"Hell if I know. Maybe they knew they were screwed for

losing the chief's son so they just did their own running, in the opposite direction."

Hannah thought about Laurel's theory, which made some sense. She didn't know enough about Sef's son, but if he was anything like the nobles' kids, it wouldn't be too farfetched.

"Maybe. Every one of those noble kids were worthless," she sighed.

"That's what I hear," Laurel agreed.

"Especially Gregory…"

"Hey!" Laurel shouted, giving Hannah a shove. "And I was thinking about taking back that whore comment, but you can forget about that."

"So, what's the deal there? You seem awfully smitten with that nerd. Must not be many guys back in the Forest."

Laurel smiled. "There are plenty of guys where I come from— you could say they… *grow on trees.*"

Hannah rolled her eyes, but smiled. "Lame."

"But I'll tell you what—I've never met a guy like Gregory. He's so smart. And kind. And shockingly brave for someone without a lethal bone in his body." The druid paused for a moment, staring through the leafy canopy above them. "But he's also…."

"Slow?" Hannah offered.

"Yeah. I mean, what the hell? I've been making my feelings pretty clear, right? In the Forest, if a guy liked a girl and a girl liked a guy… you know. Are guys from Arcadia not interested in… stuff like that."

Hannah thought about Parker for a second, and felt the warmth rising on her cheeks. She coughed, "No, they definitely are. Gregory's just a gentleman. He doesn't want to rush things. Doesn't want to hurt you."

"Hurt me?" Laurel opened her eyes in shock. "You'd think for how smart he is, he'd know by now I'm not that fragile."

Hannah thought for a second, trying to figure out what was best for her friends. "Look, I'm the last person you should be getting relationship advice from. But life is short. You should take what you want when you can. Stop waiting on that nerd and make your own move. Show him what's what."

Laurel nodded. "I just might do that."

"Listen," Hannah whispered, leaning in as they walked. "I'm going back with Aysa. Speaking as a formerly ignored member of society, I bet she knows more than Dardanus or Cal or the other asshats in the village have given her credit for. She's a good kid, and I think we connected earlier. Maybe she can fill us in a little on Samet."

Hannah dropped back again, this time to the end of the line. Aysa walked by herself, eyes locked on her boots. "What are you doing way back here?" Hannah asked.

The girl shrugged. "It's kind of my normal spot. Actually, a lot closer than normal. I don't really belong with them." She nodded toward the soldiers.

"Damn, girl, the way you fought back there? Your ass totally belongs anywhere you want it to. Seriously, you've got some skills."

The girl smiled. "Thanks. I mean, I've got nothing on you. I saw that shit you pulled with the flaming vines. How the hell do you do that?"

Hannah shrugged. "Lots and lots of practice—usually when my life was on the line. Plus, I have some pretty awesome teachers."

"Your friends back in Baseek?"

Hannah nodded. "Them, and some more aboard our airship. They're some of the best people I've ever met. They would put their life on the line for me, without hesitation. And I'd do the same."

"Sounds pretty nice. Sorry for freaking out and attacking you when I first saw you."

Hannah gave her a playful punch on the arm. "No worries. I'd have done the same. I mean, we must look pretty weird to you all."

Aysa grinned. "Well, you do have some stumpy little legs. Especially the old fart. And your weird little hands. How do you even hold anything?"

"Screw you," Hannah laughed. "My hands are dainty, thank you very much. And it's not like I need to throw heavy rocks like you, not when I can toss a few fireballs around."

Aysa fell quiet for a second, then met Hannah's eyes. "Tell me more... about your magic. Did you have to make a deal with the devil or something?"

Hannah smiled, remembering Zeke's face on the first day she met him.

"Something like that. If we make it through this, I promise I'll tell you all about it. It's one heck of a story. But I've got a couple questions for you. Samet's disappearance... I don't know. Could he have run away or something? I don't know the kid at all, so it's kind of hard to imagine the whole thing and how it might've gone down. What's he like?"

The girl flushed a bright pink, and Hannah knew that she saw him as more than just a confidante. Hannah wondered how he viewed the relationship.

"Sam was the only person who ever treated me like I wasn't invisible... or worse, just a drain on Baseek. He wasn't just kind for the sake of being kind; I think he really liked me. Sometimes, he would sneak out, and we'd run up to the cliffs and just lay there counting stars and talking about what the world might be like beyond the coast." She laughed. "Just dumb kid stuff, I guess. But it wasn't serious. No way he'd take off. He's Sef's son. He'll lead Baseek one day. He wouldn't just abandon that."

"You sure?" Hannah asked.

"What do you mean?"

"Look, I'm just weighing all the options. It's a big world out there

—believe me. And you said it yourself, it can kind of suck living in one place your whole life. If you could just drop everything and go right now on a grand adventure, wouldn't you at least be tempted?"

Aysa thought for a second before shaking her head. "I couldn't leave Sam. And he wouldn't leave me—not without telling me first."

They dropped down a steep slope and then rose even higher on the other side. They were getting close to Kofken and nearly on the site where the roamers had seen the Baseeki guards.

Hannah knew she didn't have much more time with just Aysa, and her next question was a little sensitive in nature. "So, it sounds like you two are pretty close. You spent a lot of time with Sam, right?"

"Yeah. Guess so."

"And with his guard?"

The girl laughed. "Well, of course. Except for when we snuck away, the guard was always with him. Chief Sef is a cautious man, and there's a lot of bad out here. Sam couldn't take a shit without someone standing over him with a set of bolas in their hand."

Hannah giggled. "There are so many jokes I want to make right now... Anyway, so they were good men? The guys who were with him when he went missing?"

"That I don't really know. It was a new group guarding him."

Hannah stopped dead in her tracks. "Wait. What?"

"Yeah. Emen—that guy we found with his head bashed in—was the only regular. It was usually just him watching Sam, but then they decided to up his security detail. Added some elite forces to the mix. With all the rumors of the Kofkens and a possible attack, I guess it was to make sure Sam was safe." She waved her arms out toward their surroundings. "And here we are."

"Indeed," Hannah sighed thinking of this new twist on things. "I guess Sef is really overprotective."

Aysa nodded. "You can say that again." She continued walking, and Hannah fell in beside her. "But it wasn't the chief who assigned the new guard. It was Vatan."

"Vatan? She's got that kind of power? I thought she was Sef's mistress or something."

Aysa laughed again. "No way. She's basically the number two back at home. Has been for years."

Before Hannah could ask another question, Dardanus yelled from in front of them. "Hannah. Get your ass up here! You gotta see this."

CHAPTER FOURTEEN

Attack was the last thing the remnant expected, which gave Gregory the only edge he had. He dropped his shoulder, his small frame carrying enough momentum to bowl a few over. The surprise attack gave him a little space to maneuver, and he swung his wrench wildly back and forth, trying to keep them at bay.

It worked—for about two seconds.

The remnant were just too fierce, and they had him surrounded. Another ten were advancing from every direction. Gregory held his wrench out in front of him in vain, turning and pointing it at each of the remnant.

"Stay back you bastards or I'll, I'll, tear you to pieces!"

His threats only made them laugh harder.

"Sal!" he shouted, hoping the dragon might be of some assistance.

But, the dragon had his hands full. A half dozen remnant were attacking from each side. As he swiped away one with his powerful tail, another took his place. Talons ripped remnant flesh, but the men, mad with murder on their minds, advanced until their bodies could do no more.

Each time he tried to take to the air, the group clung to him, dragging him back toward the dirt.

Soon enough, they would both be overtaken.

Gregory looked up at the ship one last time and thought of his father, whose hands had designed it, and his mother, who, although a terrible person, was still his mother. Finally, he thought of Hannah and Laurel. He'd miss them the most. But just the images of them gave him courage.

Standing proudly, he screamed, "Come on! Let's do this, you bunch of filthy idiots! For Hannah!"

Saliva dripping from their filthy mouths, the remnant howled in laughter, knowing the kill was near. They walked in slowly. Delight in killing was some of the only pleasure the creatures felt in their life.

The largest of the group raised a huge club, still stained with blood from the last head she'd smashed in. The weapon hung in the air—poised to deal the finishing blow.

But it never came.

The ground quaked all around them, sending the remnant—and Gregory and Sal—to the dirt. Clouds rolled in fast from the west, covering them in unnatural darkness.

Rolling to a knee, Gregory looked up and over his shoulder. He expected the Queen Matriarch herself to be descending from the storm, like a goddess come back to vanquish injustice.

It wasn't a god, but it was the next best thing.

Ezekiel, hair, beard, and cloak blowing in the raging wind, stood on the edge of the *Unlawful*. His staff was raised toward the heavens, and the forces of nature were bowing to his command.

"Leave my friend alone!" His shout bellowed over the storm.

He raised his staff straight in the air, and a bolt of lightning struck it. The power surged through him, and with his left hand stretched toward the ground, five bursts of lightning leapt from his fingers, leaving nothing of several remnant other than burnt patches on the ground.

Gregory could hardly believe his eyes when the ancient man stepped off the ship. He drifted toward the ground, landing in the center of the fray.

His body moved with the ability of a warrior half his age, his staff taking out remnant after remnant. Blue bolts of power killing the others. He whipped around, eyes blazing red, and pushed an orb of power into the circle surrounding Gregory. With a clap, the orb burst, destroying half of the enemy.

Gregory ducked for cover, trying not to be hit by the bits of remnant bodies exploding into the sky.

"Damn," he whispered.

Most of the remnant stared in awe, but two bold fighters attacked him from the rear. As their swords swung for their target, Ezekiel disappeared with a whoosh of wind. They screamed in unison, both of them impaled on the other's' weapon.

Reappearing yards away, the magician went back to work. With bolts of power and tongues of flame, he mowed down the remnant as if they were weeds in his garden. The remainder ran, charging up the hill toward the woods, in an attempt to save their lives.

But the attempt was futile.

Ezekiel closed his eyes, and when they opened, they were a darker red than Gregory had ever seen. Stretching out his arms, the old man focused on a pile of boulders at the top of hill. He clenched his fist as though he were grabbing at the air, and pulled his hand toward the sky.

Gregory watched the pile float into the air. Flicking his hands, Ezekiel mystically threw the rocks toward the retreating remnant. He directed the tiny avalanche, and there was a boulder with each of the remnants name on it.

"Holy shite," Gregory said, seeing the magician's true power for the first time.

As the last screams faded, the storm dissipated, and the hillside once again became quiet, like nothing at all had happened.

Ezekiel's eyes went back to normal, and he leaned on the staff, letting the tension from the fight leave his body. "Well," he finally said, "all those days cooped up in my room. It's nice to get out and stretch my legs."

"That. Was. *Amazing.*"

Ezekiel grinned and gave a slight bow.

"But how did you…"

The old man laughed as Sal ran over to him. Reaching down, he scratched under the dragon's jaw.

"How did I know you were in trouble? Easy. I asked for absolute quiet. And in the middle of my trance, I noticed that there wasn't a sound."

Gregory shook his head. "But that's what you asked for."

"Exactly. And when have you lot ever done what I asked? I knew straight away that disaster must have struck. So, he said, looking around. "Anything interesting going on?"

Gregory couldn't stand it any longer. He fell to the ground laughing.

With that, Ezekiel rolled his eyes and walked off toward the rope ladder.

Gregory finally regained his breath, and Sal curled up next to him. He and the dragon had never been closer.

"I don't know, Sal. I think we could have taken them," he said, then burst into laughter once again.

"What the hell do you mean I was looking at your girl?" Hadley shouted at the top of his lungs. "I didn't even know you had a girl!"

The porter looked up from his book, and then back down. He'd seen more than one brawl behind the bars, and this was nothing new. Tempers rose when people were locked up, especially if those people were fed a constant stream of intoxicating beverage.

Parker's face dropped in shock. "Didn't know?"

"No."

"How could you not know she was my girl? Are you a freaking idiot or what?"

"Or what." Hadley grinned. "I mean, I knew you two were friends, and… She is pretty damned hot, but I've never seen you make a move or show any kind of affection or anything."

"The hell, Hadley?" Parker screamed, his voice ramping up the decibels. "We've basically been side-by-side since we were babies!"

Hadley raised his brows. "Huh. I never thought of it like that. I thought you were her…"

"Her what?" Parker yelled, his face grew red, and his tone drew the porter's attention again.

"You know, I thought you were her *gay* friend. I mean, they all have one, right?" Hadley shrugged. "Listen, I don't judge, pal. It's not like we're living before the Age of Madness after all. I thought she was fair game. Besides, I'm pretty sure she's into me."

The two stared each other down, and the porter stood, realizing some shit was about to go down. The rearick was snoring loudly, as if nothing at all was happening—which meant he would be no help. Opening the door, the porter motioned for a guard just outside the jail room to join him. He was going to need back up.

"You mean, you're not gay?" Hadley asked just as they returned.

"You son of a bitch!" Parker roared. He snapped and rushed the mystic, slamming him against the hard, stone walls.

He continued his attack with several blows to Hadley's chest, eliciting sharp cries from the mystic.

"Get that door open!" the guard shouted to the porter, who was already fumbling with his keys.

They rushed past the sleeping rearick and grabbed the men, knowing if Parker had much more time, he would tear his cellmate to pieces. It took both of them to pull the Arcadian off the mystic. Just as they broke up the fight, a loud voice behind them said, "Sorry, lads."

Karl crashed his mug into the back of the guard's head, dropping him to the floor.

"Seems like a waste of good brew if you ask me," Karl said, looking at the shattered cup.

Hadley looked up at the porter, whose eyes were now wide with fear. Their ruse had become perfectly clear to him, but it was too late to do anything about it. The mystic's eyes turned white, and he placed a hand on the Baseeki man's shoulder. "You're feeling ridiculously tired. This whole ordeal has worn you out. You should sleep now."

He nodded, walked to Parker's cot, and crawled in.

"See, rearick, barbarism isn't always called for," he said to Karl.

"Aye," Karl snorted, "if ya think scramblin' a man's brains is civilized, then I'd hate to see ya really mad. Anyway, bet mine stays out longer." He looked down at the unconscious guard, then back at the two young men. "I don't mean ta be a critic, but that little show you two put on. A little close to home don't ya think?"

Parker shrugged. "I couldn't pull my punches, not if we wanted it to be realistic. But I didn't know what he was going to come up with for us to act out."

"Who was acting?" Hadley asked.

"Screw you," Parker said. "And for the record, I'm not gay."

Hadley stood, smiling smugly, "You lowlanders and your labels. In my experience, we shouldn't limit love. Just be honest with yourself, Park."

Parker rolled his eyes. "Karl, can you—"

Karl put up his hands. "Not gettin' in the middle of this one, mates. And anyway, I need to get this bloke to bed before someone else comes lookin'. This here plan of yers still has a few other parts to be pulled off." He looked down at the body on the floor. "I'm still kinda pissed yer leaving old Karl behind, ya know."

"You're not exactly the sneaky type," Hadley said, walking for the door.

Parker followed, but then paused, looking back at Karl. "I'm not."

Karl laughed and waved him off. "Kid, you've been drooling over Hannah since the moment I met ya. Everyone knows exactly which way yer wind blows. Now, enough shit about yer preferences and get the hell outta here!"

Despite the size of the large, stone structure, it was relatively empty at this time of night. Parker and Hadley had an easy run out the back and into the shadows of Baseek. Using only the light of a half moon, they ducked down a back alley.

"No. No. No," Hadley kept saying as they ran.

"They all look the same to me. How are you going to find it?"

Hadley grinned. "Not sure. I just keep doing quick scans, trying to see if someone is talking about Vatan. You have a better idea?"

"My part was getting us out, yours is getting us in," Parker quipped. "Let's see how your superpower is going to work now."

Parker continued down the row, turned left, and stepped out toward the main path that led in front of the houses. "That one," Hadley said.

"How the…"

Hadley nodded at a man staggering down the street past the hut he had pointed to. "That guy told me. Let's just say he's having some not-so-pure thoughts about her."

Shaking his head, Parker said, "He could do that anywhere."

"Sure, but just before he stepped in front of that place, he was having impure thoughts about someone else." He pointed at the man as he moved down the row. "Ewww. You don't want to know what he's thinking about the woman in there." He slapped Parker on the back. "Superpower still working."

They strolled across the path, hoping they would make it without being noticed. Ducking into the next alley, they made their way to the back of the hut Hadley had chosen.

He laced his fingers together, offering to give Parker a boost.

"Why do I have to go first?" Parker asked.

"I'm a man of the mind. You're the big bad fighter. But don't worry, I'll be out here meditating... and thinking about your girlfriend."

Parker gave him a jab on the shoulder. "She's not my girlfriend."

"Of course, she's not. Like she'd ever have you," Hadley said with half a grin. "Now, get your ass in there and then haul me up."

Lifting himself up, Parker peered into the room. The place was dark, with only a little moonlight splashed through the windows. But as far as he could tell, nobody was home. He held his breath, and gave the window a push. Effortlessly, it slid open, granting him entrance. He pulled himself up and over the sill, onto the floor. He froze, listening for movement, but he heard nothing.

"Thanks, comrade," Hadley said once Parker hauled him up and into the room. "Now, let's see what we can find?"

"Yeah, um, what are we looking for anyway?"

"Dunno. Maybe a journal where she writes about the fact that she is a really bad person, bent on torturing Karl, and taking over the universe."

Parker walked across the room, his eyes adjusting to the lack of light. "I'll keep my eyes out for that."

They scoured the bedroom, which was nearly devoid of anything but the bed, and then moved into the open living room and kitchen area. Also, empty. There wasn't much for them to search other than a few notes on parchment about nothing at all, dishes, and a lumpy couch.

"She's probably a lot of fun to hang out with," Hadley quipped taking in the bare essentials.

"This is weird."

"Yeah, like she just moved in, or something," Hadley said, pulling open empty drawers and shutting them again.

"Or... she's moving out."

They both froze as they heard the sound of footsteps outside.

"Shit," Parker whispered. "Go!"

The door swung open before they could reach the window. Even if they did make it out of the room, any detection would be bad for Hannah and likely death for Karl.

Silently, they chose another path. They dropped to the floor and rolled under the bed.

"How cliche," Hadley whispered.

Parker only gave him a jab in the ribs.

Footsteps moved about the house. The quiet sound of humming—a joyful song—came from the other room. Vatan—or whoever it was—was really quite pleased with the evening.

She walked in, and Parker could see large bare feet move across the floor. They were definitely feminine. She stood for a minute near the corner, then Parker saw a simple cloth dress fall to the ground.

Parker looked over at Hadley who was on his back, eyes closed. He was suddenly very uncomfortable with the idea of his friend reading his thoughts.

She stepped toward them, and Parker was sure his heartbeat could be heard clear across the village. If she looked under the bed now, they would be screwed. But instead, she laid across the bed, still humming that tune.

Hadley's eyes remained closed, and Parker prayed the mystic had something up his sleeve.

After what felt like an eternity of tense silence and trying not to breath, the Baseeki woman rose to her feet and chose another outfit. She dressed quickly, then walked out the way she came.

When he thought it was safe, Parker exhaled. "Holy shit. Was that her?" Parker whispered.

"Oh, yeah."

"And…"

"And… We're in big trouble," Hadley said. "We need to get the hell out of here."

"Why? What was she thinking about?" Parker asked.

"Murder."

CHAPTER FIFTEEN

Karl sat on his cot with the guard and the porter under the blankets on his friends' beds. It wasn't a great disguise—considering the Baseeki were both almost a foot taller than Parker and Hadley, but it was the best they could come up with. If it was discovered that the two young men were out sneaking around, the village would erupt.

Karl watched carefully as the door opposite his cell opened. Parker's plan was about to be put to the test.

As the guard entered, Karl began singing an old folk song from the Heights. The mug in his hand had been empty for hours, but he hoped the prop would be effective. Adding a belch into his repertoire for good measure, Karl smiled wide.

The guard crinkled his nose in disgust.

"Ah, you're piss drunk, rearick. Why don't you sleep like your friends?" He stopped and looked around. "Where the hell is the porter, and the man I'm supposed to be replacing?"

Karl stretched his mug in his direction. "I've been wonderin' the same damn thing fer nearly an hour. I'm nearly out." He motioned to his friends' spots. "Drank them two under the table hours ago. Care to have a spot with me?"

The man's face crinkled again and Karl wondered if it was a medical condition.

"No, I don't want to drink with you." He paused, as the unconscious guard started to move and moan under his sheet.

Karl froze. He had lost the bet with Hadley; his guy was definitely coming to first—and far too soon.

Nodding toward the unconscious guard, the replacement asked, "Is something wrong with him?"

"Ha ha he's just a pisser!" Karl yelled. "It's alright then, if ye don't wanna drink with me. Drinkin' alone is just as good anyway. Have yerself a good evening," Karl said more quickly than he had meant to.

The guard looked suspiciously at Karl, who had never been very good at acting—or lying—and then over at the man on the bed.

"Shit. The chief will have my ass if one of you chokes on your vomit." The guard pulled a key from his pocket and approached the bars.

"Scheisse, man, those Arcadians can drink like fish, but they sleep like cats. Don't worry 'bout a thing. I'll watch 'em."

He ignored Karl and swung the gate open. Striding across the cell, he pulled on the sheet, exposing the guard, half-conscious and bound to the rails of the cot. Turning, he opened his mouth to say something to the drunk rearick. Before he could, a mostly sober Karl caught him with a fist in the stomach, and then another across the face.

Karl looked down at the unconscious man, then scanned the room. "Well, hell. What am I gonna do with another one of them?"

Laurel was already poking around the scene by the time she and Aysa arrived. Gathered in a circle on the edges, the men watched her careful work, making comments of admiration—mostly about her skills.

One of the men made a comment about the curve of her ass just as Hannah arrived.

"Careful," she said, "her boyfriend is freaking enormous and eats pricks like you for breakfast."

His eyes grew big. "Really?"

She snorted as she laughed. "Nah. He's actually a skinny, little nerd. He wouldn't hurt a fly. I, on the other hand, will incinerate you if you even think another thought about my friend's ass. And trust me, I'll know." Her eyes flashed red as she spoke, and the man's face turned pale.

"Shit. Sorry," he mumbled. "And... sorry for those other thoughts, too."

Hannah slapped him on the arm. "Good boy. Gotta treat the Arcadian Valley girls with respect, or you'll get your balls stomped." She gave him a seductive wink and watched as his eyes opened in terror.

Laughing, she joined Laurel. "Whatta ya got?"

"Nearly the same as the last time. Not much of a struggle, if any at all. Nothing that raises too much suspicion." Laurel crouched at the base of a tree. "Except these."

She picked up short lengths of rope. They had knots in them, but were sliced in half by a serrated knife.

"They were tied up here?" Hannah pointed at the tree.

Laurel tilted her head. "Just one person—probably Samet. Still no sign of his guards." Nodding to the eastern side of the clearing, she said, "They left that way. I checked, but the trail disperses. No idea if they were truly heading toward Kofken or somewhere else. There's a four-way intersection in the trail ahead, they could have travelled further east and down to Kofken. Or they could have doubled back to keep us running in circles."

"Damn," Hannah said, making a fist by her side. "Wish I had some sort of magic that could track them."

Laurel laughed. "You do, girlfriend. Just haven't learned this one yet. Watch. And take notes." She jabbed Hannah playfully on the shoulder. "Always wanted to say that to you."

The druid dropped to her knees, sitting on her heels. Palms up in her lap, she closed her eyes and started muttering. As she did, the hidden animal world around them exploded. A flock of birds swooped in, dipped and then flew out of sight. A little animal—something that looked like a groundhog—scurried across the clearing. Even the bugs started chirping, screaming their allegiance.

Laurel continued until a she wolf, with one gray-blue eye and one brown, crept out of the woods. Without looking at any of the other humans, she walked straight to Laurel and rested her head on the druid's lap. Bending, Laurel wrapped her arms around the creature, her eyes covered over with green.

The rest of the group stood still, trying not to draw the animal's attention.

After a moment, the wolf rose and turned for the cut vines. She sniffed and walked around the tree several times before trotting out to the spot where the group had left the clearing.

"We have a new member of our team," Laurel smiled. "She reminds me of one of the warrior's wolves in the Forest. Luna. She'll be more help to us than anything else."

"*And* she's a lot smarter than the lot of you," Hannah said nodding at Dardanus and his men.

He chuckled at her jab this time. "We'll see, Arcadian."

They sped off down the trail after the wolf, a creature much faster than any of them. Every hundred yards or so, she would turn and wait, long pink tongue hanging from her mouth.

It wasn't far before they hit the intersection Laurel had described, where four well-worn paths split, one in each direction. The wolf walked in circles, sniffing each trail several times.

She turned her head toward Laurel, multi-colored eyes blinking, before she took off down the path that continued east.

"She wants us to wait," Laurel said.

"Bullshit," said one of the men. "Just some stray mutt."

Laurel grinned. "She'll be back. And call her that again, and I imagine that mutt might just show you what she's made of."

He glanced up at Dardanus, who gave a shake of his head. The man slunk to the back of the line.

A few minutes later, Laurel's friend returned, nose in the ground once again before she chose her path. Taking several strides, she turned and howled into the air.

"She's got it." Laurel beamed with pride and took off after the wolf. The others continued on her heels.

"Damn it," Dardanus grumbled.

Hannah asked what troubled him.

"That's the path to Kofken. All this time I had convinced myself that it couldn't be them, that all the talk about the tribe and its violence against Baseek was just that—talk. But if that wolf is right…"

"Our priority is to find the kid. We'll deal with whatever we find when we get there."

The ground beneath them grew rocky, and the path began its long descent into Kofken. After only a minute, the village came into sight. Rows and rows of tiny huts, all aligned perfectly, led toward the sea. In the middle, a building stood, bigger and grander than the others. If Hannah didn't know better, she'd swear she was walking right back into Baseek. From this distance, they could have been identical.

She stumbled down the path behind the Baseeki, who seemed to effortlessly glide over the rough terrain. They stopped short, and she nearly took one out since she was watching her damned feet to keep from stumbling over the rocks.

"You guys need a break, huh?" she asked, sweat dripping down her face. "I get it. Not everybody can dance through a mountain path like I can." She breathed hard through pursed lips, sending a tendril of her bangs up and off her forehead. No matter the reason, she was glad for a short rest.

"We didn't stop," Dardanus replied. "She did." He pointed at the wolf who sat in the middle of the path.

Laurel bent down to her and whispered in her pointed ears. As she stood, the wolf cut off the trail, leaping between rocks as she made her own path.

"They didn't go to the village," Laurel said, pointing in the direction of the wolf navigating the terrain. "Turned off the path here. My friend has their scent, and it looks like a small group passed through here not long ago."

"Why the hell would they do that?" the mouthy guard asked. The other nodded along with him. "They got the boy. Made it this far. Why not just descend into the city?"

"He's right, screw the animal. We need to get down there immediately before they hurt him." Dardanus's face was stern and resolved.

"I'm not screwing the animal," Hannah quipped. "An Arcadian would never..."

"You know that's not what I meant."

Hannah laughed. "Lighten up, D, before you hurt someone. It's stupid to go charging in guns blazing. None of this adds up. We should tread lightly."

The men looked back and forth, trying to figure out who to follow. Dardanus was their leader, but Hannah had showed herself to be quite the badass.

The tall man crossed his arms. "Listen—"

"No, you listen." Hannah cut him off with the wave of her hand. "You may have forgotten that my life, and the life of my friends is riding on this. Like it or not, we're a team out here. I have my magic, charm, and stunning good looks. You guys have your height and your little balls." She pointed to the bola hanging from his belt and winked. "But Laurel, she's got all of this natural world around us speaking to her. And right now, she has that wolf leading the way. It's time you drop the controlling leader thing, if only for one more day, and trust us."

"And why the hell should we trust you?" the second in command asked.

"Well, we got you this far, did more than our fair share against those roamers, saved one of your men from certain death... other than that, I've got nothing. You march into the middle of town, and Samet is there, they'll kill him in an instant. And then kill you. Let's give Laurel her shot. If he's not there, we take the night and make a plan. Remember what would have happened if you rushed that group back there? You'd be having a lot more hard conversations with mourning wives when you got home. Get the picture?"

Dardanus held his second's arm, holding him back from responding. "We will follow you, Hannah from Arcadia. But I swear, if this turns to shit, it won't just be your life on the line."

"Yeah, yeah. I've heard it all before. Let's just do this."

The group headed up the path with Laurel in the lead. Aysa walked close to Hannah, perfectly comfortable finding her own path. "There's a hut up here."

"No shit?"

She shook her head. "None. Abandoned, though. It was built early on, high on the rocks as a watchtower while the town was being founded."

"Sounds like a good place to hide a prince."

Aysa nodded. "Bad part is, they can see all around from there. They probably know we're coming."

"Got it."

"And the Kofken are really good at throwing rocks."

"Got that, too," Hannah nodded.

"And the climb gets steeper at the end, the approach will be nearly impossible if we're attacked."

"And… got it." Hannah scanned the rocks above, but all she saw was more of them. "So, you're saying we're screwed?"

"An oldtimer from Baseek used to have a saying about rowing up shit creek without a paddle…"

Hannah shook her head. "Great."

They continued up the path. At one high point, Hannah could swear she made out the roof of a building in the distance, but it disappeared when they dipped into a tiny saddle that sat between the rises.

She stayed on high alert, ready to throw a shield if necessary. Although they'd done nothing but hike since the battle below, she knew that some of her strength had returned. Probably not enough to pull off anything too heroic. She wished there was time for a steak dinner, a hot bath, and a feather bed to really amp her up. But those things were likely out of the question.

Catching up with Laurel, who was moving quickly through the boulders, even with her wounded leg, Hannah pulled on her sleeve. "Listen. There's a hut ahead, some sort of outpost. I bet my magic they're keeping little Sammie there. Be on high alert."

Laurel brow was knit with concern. "Got it. But I'll tell you the truth. I don't have much left in the tank."

"I hear you. But we can always dig deeper." Hannah cursed as her foot slipped, ramming her shin into a rock.

"Yeah. I keep telling myself that," Laurel replied.

As they wove through a pile of giant rocks that jutted from the ground, Laurel's wolf howled out a warning.

"They know we're here," Laurel whispered.

"If they didn't before…"

Laurel laughed. "I know what that howl means, Hannah. She's telling us someone is waiting for us at the top."

Dardanus crouched next to them. "I'm going first."

"Like hell you—"

He interrupted Hannah's dispute. "Arcadian, where you come from you have fought battles for your people, your place. Important battles. Is that right?" She nodded silently. "And if some shit-talking guard from Baseek came and wanted to lead you into the last moments of those battles, would you step aside and let him take both danger and tribal pride away from you?"

"Not a noble's chance in the Boulevard."

He cocked his head to the side. "I'll take that as a no. Now, you understand. I need to go first. It must be me."

"I'm going to be right behind you," she replied.

He nodded gravely. "I sure as hell hope so. Now, let's go."

Dardanus gave his men and the other women the command to wait behind cover, they grumbled but complied as he slid out from behind the rocks, keeping his head low. He crept through a path his feet found faster than his mind could actually process them. Moving on this ground was second nature to him. Hannah tripped along behind him.

As they stepped out from behind the last giant boulder, a rock hummed between their heads and shattered off the rocks behind them. Hannah and Dardanus dropped to the ground.

"Stand with your hands over your head," a voice bellowed. "We are many, and our aim is true. The next shot won't be a warning."

Dardanus swallowed hard and raised his hands, standing up out of the rocks, and Hannah did the same.

"Dardanus?" the voice cried. "The hell you doing out here?"

"What do you think, Baris? I'm looking for the boy."

After an uncomfortable amount of time, Baris yelled down to them. "Shit, why you still standing there with your hands in the air. Come on up. Bring the others hiding behind the rocks, too. Samet is with us."

Dardanus exhaled. "Thank the mother." He turned and placed his hands in front of his mouth. His cheeks puffed out and a strange squawk escaped. Seconds later, the rest of his unit were coming up behind him.

They started back up the climb, Dardanus maintaining a pace

Hannah could manage, which gave the others a chance to catch up. Stepping through the last course of rocks, the watchtower came into view.

It was more of a hut, much like the ones in the village below, only more rudimentary. Looking around, she understood why the place was here. She could see a mile in every direction, and the idea that they could have snuck up on anyone paying any attention was ludicrous.

"Dardanus!" Baris gruffed, holding his arms out to his comrade.

They embraced quickly, then Dardanus stepped back. "What the hell is happening here? Where's Samet?"

"We will tell the whole tale, but first, come, come. Let us get you off your feet and something to eat. Rufus only just brought back some game and is now getting the fire ready. Then we'll tell you everything."

The head guard from Baseek nodded, his eyes dashed around the grounds surrounding the hut. Hannah's did the same. Something still felt off, but she wasn't sure quite yet what it was.

"But... Samet?" Dardanus asked as he moved toward the door.

Looking over his shoulder, Baris said, "He's inside, friend. Don't worry."

They all filed in behind Baris into the hut, which was a basic, open room. A man crouched at the fire, blowing the flames into a fire. The newly butchered animal sat on a low table next to them.

The man preparing the meat glanced over his shoulder and gave a nod to the Baseeki men and their captain. "Welcome, brothers," he said.

"Sam!" Aysa's voice sounded larger than ever in the tiny hut.

Hannah spun to find the girl leaning over a small cot in the corner. A boy, smaller than Hannah had imagined, lay on the bed. He didn't stir, and she wondered if she was looking at the prince or his corpse. Face swollen with the signs of torture, she spun, hands out ready for attack.

"Whoa!" Baris yelled. "Easy there darling. I said I would explain everything. And… Who exactly are you?"

"I'm the woman who is going to end you if you don't start explaining this shit, pronto."

He nodded, glancing back at her hands. "You're not from here, are you? You have the powers?"

"More than you can imagine, douche nugget, and if you don't want a firsthand display, start talking. What'd you do to the boy?" Her eyes narrowed on him, watching every move.

"Dard, can you call off your attack dog, please?" Baris laughed nervously, looking toward his fellow soldier.

"Don't know, friend. I might be with her on this one. Looks awfully suspicious to me." Dardanus eased his hand down to the rope of his bolas, waiting for a response.

The man's eyes cut to Dardanus's hand, ready for action and back to Hannah. He raised his hands. "I don't want any trouble here. Just doing my job."

"Your job," Aysa shouted from across the room, "was to protect him."

Baris cast the one-armed girl a look of disdain. Hannah could tell he didn't like her, but according to Aysa, no one did. She took a second to nudge Laurel in the ribs, nodding toward the man by the fire. Her friend gave a slight tilt of her head, and kept her eye on the second guard.

Looking down at the dirt floor, Baris's face filled with embarrassment. "She's right," he said, pointing to Aysa. "It was my job —our job. Hell, we've been watching the kid for weeks; easiest assignment of my life. In fact—" his eyes wandered to each of the guests in the hut "—I wondered why the hell Vatan put us on babysitting duty." He looked at Dardanus. "I mean, no offense, but our skills could be used in a lot better ways."

Dardanus clenched his jaw, showing self-control. "None taken. Yet. Go on."

"We brought the little brat up to the spot above our village.

Kid wanted to go there almost every day. Rufus and I were just chilling under a tree when the arrow came in."

"Kofken arrow," Dardanus's second chimed in. "We saw it in the tree."

"Yeah," Baris laughed. "Better the tree than in my ass. We hit the ground and returned a little fire up into the crags, but when we were sure the coast was clear, the damned kid was gone. We tracked them for the better part of the day until we came upon the site, just down the trail from here."

"He was tied up," Dardanus said, seeing where the story was leading.

"Yeah. And beat to hell from what we could see. Not sure why they stopped where they did, maybe they wanted to bring the enemy home to their people truly vanquished, but they went further than they should have, I imagine."

Hannah could feel the men from Baseek relax around her, but something still didn't feel right. She wanted the rest of the story. "How'd you free him?"

"You're not the only one with powers, honey," Baris said with a sneer. "When we snuck up the rise, we found there were only three of 'em. Wasn't nothing for Rufus and me to give them enough of a rock shower that they decided the kid wasn't worth their lives. They turned down for the village."

Rufus, turned from the fire, and joined the conversation. "I've been up here before. My cousin, from Kofken and I would meet here and drink some swill he made in the woods. Figure we'd need to nurse him back to life, give his body a rest, before we tried getting him home."

Hannah watched the man's cheek twitch in concert with his right hand by his bola.

"Guys..." Dardanus looked down in shame. "Forgive me I thought..."

Hannah wasn't so convinced. She closed her eyes to hide their color as she cleared her mind. Rufus was certainly the weaker of the two, so she focused on his mind, tunneling her way in.

They're actually buying this shit, he thought. *Easy.*

"Yeah," Baris said. "They're planning something, Dard. The Kofken might be our family, but they aren't our friends."

"You guys are so full of shit I can smell it from here. Tell the truth, before this ends poorly," Hannah said. "I'm giving you one chance to—"

Before she could finish, Rufus pulled the device from his belt, pointing it at Dardanus, he pulled the trigger. But Hannah was ready. She flipped her wrist and threw a small shield, big enough to block the power of the blaster before it met its mark.

Rufus missed his only chance. Before he could fire again, he was screaming with his hand wrapped by Laurel's leather whip, the metal tine biting into his flesh. She pulled it hard, spinning the man off balance. Dardanus's second in command sprung to action, landing a right fist to Rufus's gut and meeting his drooping head with a knee to the chin.

"Not bad," Laurel said.

As Laurel took care of Rufus, Hannah turned toward Baris. Her eyes grew, finding the man already had Dardanus locked in a submission hold, knife on his throat.

"Don't do anything rash, you stupid witch," he hissed. "You can keep the kid, and I'll even let you have this guy back. But Rufus and I are walking out of here alive."

Hannah glanced over her shoulder at the other man in a heap on the floor. "Doesn't look like he's walking anyplace soon."

Baris looked down at the other guard and laughed. "Eh, he'd just slow me down anyway. Enough small talk. I'll drop this asshat at the bottom of the hill. You can find him there."

"And guess I shouldn't follow you? I've learned the Baseeki have good aim."

The man gave a crooked grin. "Aim? These dicks are imbeciles compared to me."

Hannah smiled. "You know who else has good aim?"

"Who?" he asked, with a look of confusion.

"She does." Hannah motioned to Laurel, who didn't hesitate.

Before Baris could even shift the blade at Dardanus's neck, her rope was wrapped around his forearm. Straining, Laurel pulled it away.

With the enemy's blade out of harm's way, Hannah pulled her own, and threw it, trusting in the training she had received from Karl.

Inches from Dardanus's face, the blade sunk into Baris's eye. The traitor reached for its hilt. No sooner had he grabbed it than he hit the ground, dead.

"Bullseye," Laurel said with a giggle. "Get it? *Bullseye.*"

Hannah looked over at her, heart still racing. "Oh, I definitely get it."

CHAPTER SIXTEEN

"What the hell is going on here?" Cal shouted as he watched Baris's blood spill onto the floor.

Dardanus raised a hand, his eyes on Hannah and Laurel leaning over Samet. "Seems we found our prince and his captors. But you need to hold your tongue so they can concentrate. The boy is in bad condition. Death is on the doorstep, and the magicians are trying to tell him he isn't welcome here."

After ten minutes, give or take, Laurel collapsed onto the floor, exhausted. Hannah soon followed.

"It's all I have," the druid said.

Hannah nodded. "Me, too." She turned to Dardanus. "He's not good, but stable for now. I need some rest, as does Laurel. Not to mention that you and your men look almost as bad as the kid here."

"And you'll be able to heal him in the morning?"

She shook her head. "No. I've taken him as far as I can, but I know someone who can help."

They all found a spot on the dirt floor and covered themselves with whatever they could find.

Aysa crawled over to Hannah's side. "I'll keep first watch. You sleep."

Hardly able to nod, Hannah thanked her.

"No. Thank you... for Sam."

The magician considered saying "you're welcome," but she was asleep before the words could form on her lips.

Hadley dropped from the window and landed in the grass next to Parker. Silently, they sped for the back pathways they had originally come from. Once safely away from Vatan's hut, they took a breather and leaned against a small shed, out of sight from the main path.

"Damn, that was intense!" Hadley said. "We barely made it out of there."

"I agree it was a skin of our teeth moment, but you probably could have done something, right?"

"Yeah," he said, rolling his eyes, "but our folks don't know that. Let's make this story the best we can for the others."

Parker laughed. "All right, you can work on our tall tale while I work on a way to save the day. So, what exactly did she say in her head?"

Laughing, Hadley said, "What do you say in your head?"

Parker sat staring without a response.

"What I mean is, people don't really think like that, you know, in words. At least that's not how I see them. It's almost always pictures."

"OK, so, what pictures did you see in her head?"

Hadley shifted on the hard ground. "Nothing much. Just the chief being killed over and over and over again. Mix that with her joyful humming, and you get the picture. I don't think she's currently very concerned for his wellbeing."

"Shit. Me neither. We better get over there."

Without waiting for Hadley's response, Parker rose and crept through the shadows, toward Sef's house. Compared to the way Adrien had lived in Arcadia, Sef's place was humble, although it was a little bigger than the rest of the simple huts. They got within a block before Parker pulled up short, Hadley slamming into his back.

"What is it?"

"Look." Parker pointed toward the men, ten strong, surrounding the hut. "And that's just what we can see. They must be on high alert. I'm guessing because of Samet."

"Or they know something we don't. If Vatan is part of some coup, we don't really know who to trust."

Parker shrugged. "Either way, it's unlikely we will be able to walk right in, unless you can zap us inside."

Hadley smirked and shook his head. "You're really clueless about how all this works still, aren't you? I can project my mind and image. Can't teleport. That's your people."

"So, that time you were perving out and looking at Hannah naked, you were actually doing it from another room. I think that might just be creepier."

Shaking his head, Hadley said, "I've made it clear, I didn't see a thing… But I've got a great imagination."

"All right, Captain Perv, I've got a plan, but we're going to need some help. I'll tell you on the way."

───

Parker slammed through the door, fists up and ready for a fight, but his offensive posture was uncalled for. His jaw dropped as he saw Karl sitting on his cot, surrounded by a half-dozen unconscious guardsmen. The two strapped to the beds were squirming.

He took a sip of his drink and shrugged. "What can I say? I'm not a very good prisoner, and them bastards just kept coming!"

Hadley crossed the room and grabbed Karl's hammer off the top shelf, he threw it to the rearick who fastened it to his hip. "So, what's the plan? If it involves me using this, I'm in."

Parker smiled. "You may come to regret that. Come on. I'll tell you on the way."

They raced out of the main building and toward the alleyway leading to Sef's house. As they walked in the shadows, Parker filled him in on the events of the evening, including the visual Hadley had of Vatan and the chief.

Karl snorted as they got close to their target. "Damn! Well, guess we're gonna be damned heroes after all. I'm glad ya got me before breakin' the news to Chief Longarms. I can't wait to see the look on his face when we tell 'em the shadow shit was against 'em all the time."

"Yeah... about that," Hadley said, trailing off in hopes that Parker would break the news.

Parker grinned, glad to be the bearer of their plan. "We need you to make a distraction so we can get inside."

Karl looked back and forth at the two men. "What the hell are ye talkin' about? And why me?"

"Cause you're good at being a spectacle," Parker said. "And, anyway, if they catch you, you'll be able to kick their asses. I'd hardly stand a chance, and Hadley here would only try to amuse them with pictures of dancing girls or something. Come on. We need you on this one."

"Scheisse, ya bloody bastards."

"Just need you to distract them, Karl. Let us slip in," Hadley urged him. "We might need my powers of persuasion once we're through the doors."

"Aye, I know you two are a couple a weak twats... Guess I can. But I don't like yer plans. Always have me hangin' my ass out."

Parker cocked his head to the side. "We didn't think of the ass thing, but that would probably do the trick."

"Bite me, Arcadian."

Parker's face grew serious. "Thanks, Karl. And be safe."

Karl grunted. "Aye, ya don't get to my age fightin' safe. But I should be able to lead those bastards on a merry chase. Don't waste my sacrifice!"

Without waiting for another word, the rearick grabbed the hammer from his belt and walked straight for the chief's front door, whistling a rearick wedding song. All eyes were on him. The guards slapped each other's arms, murmuring and wondering what the hell they should do.

"Aye, Baseeki bastards, I came to offer me apology. Not sure what happened, but I think I broke yer jail… and a few skulls while I was at it."

The guard standing directly in front of Sef's front door shouted back, "Drop the hammer, rearick. There are too many of us. The chief commanded us to play it nice, but if you don't comply, we'll take you by force."

Karl laughed as loud as he could. "Take me? It's gonna take longer arms then yers to catch me!" Karl spun his hammer in arcs in front of him. "Hey, I talked with one of them ladies of yers. She said the Matriarch gave ya those long strong arms 'cause ya spent most yer time jerking off. Is that right?"

"We warned you!" the head guard shouted. "Let's get him."

The others screamed their assent, and the men rushed Karl.

Swinging the hammer left and right, he dropped the first three that approached with ease. Kicking the next back into the group, he turned and ran for the shadows, yelling, "Come on, ya bastards, unless ya need to stop and churn the butter!"

Hadley nudged Parker. "He's good at bugging the hell out of people."

Laughing, Parker said, "Yeah, a little too good. We'd better hurry."

Hannah watched the Baseeki men descend the rocky trail carrying Samet on a stretcher. They made it from materials scavenged from the building overlooking Kofken. Even with the weight and the rocks, they were more agile than Hannah. She felt like a drunk from Sully's on his way home after an all-night bender.

"How the hell do you guys do that?" she asked Dardanus, who was nearly floating over the stones in front of her.

"What? Walk?" He laughed. "We've been doing it all of our lives." Slapping his long legs, he added, "And, you could say we were made for this."

"Guess you're the opposite of the rearick."

"Yeah," he said. "We wouldn't be much use underground in their mines, that's for sure. Nature makes us the way she needs us."

"And the nanocytes don't hurt either," she mumbled, knowing more of the story of their evolution than they themselves knew.

"What's that?"

"Nothing," she said, not feeling like giving a science lesson. They walked in silence a little longer, and she could tell his heart was heavy. "You feeling alright? We're bringing Samet home. My friend can help him, I know it. He's going to be OK."

He glanced over his shoulder, forcing a smile. "No. I mean, yes, that is very good. It was our mission after all, but Baris and Rufus... The guard, we're all like brothers. I just don't understand how they could do that. And why? What were they after?"

"I don't know. But I bet Samet can tell us more once he comes to."

He continued down the path for several strides before continuing. "Maybe. But I've gotta talk to the chief. We still don't know what's up with Kofken, why they've done this and what they want. I thought we were a team, a family. Working together to hold on to what little peace we've found. Now, it looks like that's all going up in smoke."

They reached the top of a small rise. Off to the right, the sea spread out beneath them. Baseek sat on its edge, looking peaceful from their vantage point as if no one knew anything about what was happening above them.

"That's where we're going," Hannah said, pointing to their left. Their ship was on the patch of green where Gregory had left them, only a few hundred yards off. "That's where help is."

Dardanus didn't say a word, he just stared at the massive arc. Hannah didn't need to be able to read minds to know what the big man was thinking.

War is hell. Even more so when your enemy is family.

Hannah squeezed his shoulder, trying to give comfort, if only a little. "The man inside that ship, Ezekiel, he is probably the most powerful wizard that has ever lived."

"You told me he will heal Samet."

Hannah's smile cracked through her sadness for him. "Yes. He will heal Samet, but that's not all. We are on a journey that will take us far from here. A pilgrimage. And when we get to our destination, the man inside that ship is going to make everything right. With the help of a friend, he's going to heal all of Irth."

He nodded. "Just like in the stories."

She narrowed her eyes. "What stories?"

"The ones we heard when we were young, about a world reborn from the fire."

"Yeah," Hannah said. "Something like that. We might be walking through the coals now, but it's only making us stronger. Who knows? Maybe one day your strength will win you the peace you're looking for."

Standing in the shadow of the ship, Hannah counted bodies of fallen remnant. She got to twenty-five before Aysa pulled on her sleeve.

"What the hell happened here?"

Hannah whistled. "Looks like Ezekiel happened here."

Laurel dramatically cleared her throat loudly enough for all to hear.

'And I'm sure our friend Gregory probably took one out, too. Probably that small one over there." Hannah pointed. "The one missing an eye."

Laurel grinned as Devin climbed out of her cloak and sat on her shoulder. "You should know that Gregory basically runs the entire ship. He's the one who got us here. So, if we end up saving the world, it's because of him."

"And," Hannah jumped in, "Laurel has a big ass crush on him, so you'd better steer clear."

Aysa smiled, and her eyes cut over to Samet, still flat on the stretcher. "No problem," she said with a blush.

Nodding toward the rope ladder hanging from the ship, Hannah informed the group, "That's your way up. Samet and I will take the express route."

She bent down next to him, slid her arms carefully beneath his body, and lifted. The boy weighed less than she expected. Her eyes flashed red, and they disappeared, only a moment later to materialize on the deck of the mighty ship.

"Here you are, buddy," she said, bending down to set Samet on the floor boards. She pulled off her light jacket and slid it under his head.

Before she could stand all the way up, a green blur of scales, spikes, and wings rushed in from the stern of the ship, tackling her into a rolling ball of human and dragon.

Hannah laughed as Sal's little forked tongue licked her face over and over. "Gross!" she shouted, before pulling him into a bear hug. "Good to see you, too, you codependent little bastard. Looks like you had your way with plenty of remnant down there."

"He did," Gregory's voice said, interrupting their reunion.

Hannah leaped to her feet and ran at him, nearly taking him down with her embrace. "I missed you," she whispered into his ear. The she stepped back and grinned. "But not in some weird sexual way that would require me whispering into your ear."

He blushed. "I know. Where's—"

"Gregory!" Laurel squealed as she threw herself over the rail of the deck. She ran to him, jumping into his arms, nearly knocking him over.

He squeezed her tightly. "I was so worried about you. I'm glad you're back. I didn't know what—"

Whatever he was going to say, it got smothered by Laurel's mouth.

She leaned in and kissed him full on the lips. Hannah watched his body tighten and then relax as he kissed her back. She couldn't help smiling to herself as she watched them finally connect. Giving them their privacy, she walked toward the edge of the boat and helped Dardanus over. As soon as he stepped aboard, his eyes widened when he saw Gregory and Laurel.

"Yeah. That's been a long time coming. Give them a minute." She glanced over her shoulder and saw the two wrestling each other's faces. "Or ten."

Dardanus laughed. "Best part of coming home from battle."

"Is that right? Someone waiting for you at home right now?" Hannah asked.

He laughed harder. "Not this time. But, once I am hoisted on everybody's shoulders as a hero, I imagine I'll get some face time, too. Where's your kisser?"

"He's… I mean, um, I don't have one." Her eyes narrowed. "We women don't *need* a man, you know that, right?"

He raised his hands, worried the fireballs were coming. "Yeah, yeah. More power to you. I was just asking."

The other guards came up over the edge, landing their feet on the wooden deck, they looked around in awe. They'd seen ships on the water before, but this one looked so much more massive, sitting on the hill.

'Welcome, guys. Go ahead and hang out. Don't let those two make you sea sick," she nodded toward Gregory and Laurel, who were still at it. "Why don't you hang out with Sal here? I need to go awaken the Founder so he can come and lay his healing on Samet here."

They all stared in awe at the dragon as she walked toward the door leading down into the belly of the ship. As she moved down the thin hallway, she felt a little claustrophobic being back inside. But it also felt like home.

She stood outside of Zeke's room, listening for any movement on the other side of the door. Hadley's admonition not to disturb Ezekiel while he was trying to connect with the Oracle hung with her, and she debated knocking. If the disruption scrambled his brains, she'd never forgive herself, and she wasn't sure if she could save the world without him.

Raising her knuckles to the door, she paused one more time. The door swung open before she could knock.

"Hannah!" Ezekiel shouted. "Come on. Get the hell in here!"

His face was more filled with life than since before the battle at the tower. He looked ten years younger than when they had left from Arcadia. While she expected him to look like he had been drug through hell and back, he looked better than ever.

She dropped down into a chair by his desk. "Zeke, you're looking... damn good!" she spouted.

Laughing, he replied, "Yes, it has been sometime since I have been able to attend to myself. Ever since our early days together, I have been tapping into my energy on a consistent basis without much rest."

"But what about the Oracle?"

He sat on the edge of the bed, smoothing his robe. "That was a failure. I was unable to make a connection. It's odd, since I think we should be close enough to be in connection. But as I reach out to her, there's no response."

"Do you think she's…" Hannah left her question hanging in the air, mostly because she had no idea how to ask it. The oracle certainly wasn't human, so she was unsure if she was able to really die in a human sort of way.

"Expired?" Ezekiel asked, a sparkle in his eye. "I doubt that. Her time is limited, but she's usually pretty good on her math. She assured me she had more time, although, time is of the essence more now than ever. The clock is ticking, as they used to say. Anyway, once I realized my attempts to communicate were futile, I just took some *me* time."

Hannah laughed. "*Me time?* The hell are you, some sort of noble's mommy now?"

"Glad to see your little adventure here didn't sap all the smartass out of you!"

"It's my real magic," Hannah said.

"Well, besides a little run in with a few remnant below, I've just been resting, building my power. We're going to need it. You should take it as a piece of advice. Make sure you're continuing to meditate, rest. It will make all the difference."

Hannah nodded, but she knew that being still was the hardest part about being a magician, and she didn't really have much of a desire to navel gaze like Hadley and the mystics. She looked back up at Ezekiel. "Sure thing, boss. Now, if you're all amped up, we have a little job for you."

"Oh?"

Hannah settled into the chair to tell the story of all that had happened in Baseek and beyond during her time away from the ship. Listening well, Ezekiel would ask a question or smile and nod as if he knew all the story by heart. As far as she knew, he might have.

Getting to the present, she finally said, "Samet is up on the deck now. He's stable; Laurel and I made sure of that, but we didn't have the juice to bring him back to life—back fully, I mean."

"Yes, I see." Ezekiel stroked his beard. "Well, we wouldn't want to be bad hosts. Let's attend to the young prince."

Rising from the bed, Ezekiel led her from his little cabin up into the sunlight. The guards all milled around in a circle with Dardanus in the center near Samet. Aysa sat, rubbing Sal on the side of his head with Devin in her lap. And, Laurel and Gregory didn't quite have their faces locked together still, but they weren't far from it.

Ezekiel scanned the scene. Hannah assumed he was sweeping the minds of the newcomers. They walked to the guards, and after a brief introduction, he knelt by the boy. Placing his hands on Samet's chest, Ezekiel eyes flashed red, and immediately, the kid gasped. He sat up, his eyes wild with confusion. "No!" he screamed.

Dardanus dropped to his side. "Samet, you're OK. Everything is going to be—"

"Get away from me!" he shouted at Dardanus. "You're one of them."

"Sam!" Aysa shouted as she sprinted across the deck, with Devin spinning at her feet. She sat and drew him into an embrace. "It's OK. It's me. We found you—"

But Samet wouldn't settle. Pushing her away, his eyes turned back to Dardanus and his men. "The guards, they did this. They've turned."

Dardanus's mouth dropped open. He wanted to speak, but he knew it wouldn't do any good. Instead, Aysa continued. "It's OK. Not all of them. Not all of the guard. We found you, Sam." She nodded toward the head guard. "Dardanus saved you!"

"Like we were just along for the ride," Hannah said with a smirk before introducing herself and her crew to him.

The kid's eyes cut suspiciously back to the guard and then to his friend Aysa. Stepping in close to her, he whispered, "Don't believe them. They're all in it together. Our guard has been compromised, they've become traitors working for—"

Aysa interrupted him. "Kofken. We know. Dardanus helped to figure it out. If he were working for the other tribe we'd all be dead or behind bars."

Samet shook his head, and sat hard on the deck. "You don't understand. They weren't working for Kofken."

Dardanus's face turned grave. "What do you mean? Who was behind all of this?"

Samet looked up at the big man. "It was Vatan."

Everyone fell silent. The shock of Samet's revelation like a punch to the stomach. Finally, Hannah couldn't hold it in any longer. "That bitch!"

Aysa looked like she was going to explode. "I'll kill her!"

"But why?" Dardanus said. "I don't understand."

Samet opened his mouth, but then his face turned white. "There's no time. We have to get back to Baseek immediately. My father's life is in danger."

"*Shit*! Hannah yelled. "Vatan was 'keeping an eye' on Parker and the others. There's no telling what she did to them."

Dardanus moved to the side of the ship. The threat on his chief's life propelling him. "If we run, we can make it back to Baseek by sundown."

Hannah grabbed his shoulder. "Don't worry. You're on the *Unlawful* now. We'll make it back *well* before nightfall."

As Karl ran off into the night shouting obscenities at the men who chased him, Parker couldn't help but laugh at the rearick's creativity. He certainly invented new ways to talk about the guards' mothers. Looking back at the chief's hut, he found two men had stayed behind to protect their leader.

"Well, he cleared most of the path," he said to Hadley by his side. "But I don't expect our friend's little legs will be able to outrun the Baseeki for long. Those guys are made for speed."

"And the rearick, well, aren't." Hadley laughed. "But Karl can take care of himself. I imagine by the time they catch him, we'll either have this whole thing cleared up, or we'll be in the same kind of trouble."

Parker stood and drew his spear from his back. "Let's do this. I'll take the bigger one. Just make sure we make it as quiet as possible—don't want any additional company."

Hadley grabbed his shoulder before he could step out of the shadows of the alley. "Whatta ya say we fight smarter, not harder?"

The mystic's eyes flashed white right before he disappeared. Parker nodded and smiled. "Nice. But what about me?"

He felt a hand grip his arm. Looking down, he didn't see the arm that grabbed him—or his own.

"I wouldn't leave you out of the fun, friend," Hadley whispered. "Now, let's go. But be ready when it's time."

"How will I know it's time?"

"You'll know," Hadley said with a chuckle.

The invisible hand gave him a tug, and Parker walked, hoping they were keeping pace with one another. Crossing the quiet, village street, he couldn't help but wonder what kind of trouble he would have gotten himself into if he had the ability to disappear.

Invisibility would have certainly made their life of hustling on the streets of the Boulevard easier, granted, but no less illegal. A few other unseemly things came to mind, and he decided that the mystics were all more morally upright than he would ever be.

Just feet away from the guards, Parker could hear the men breathing as their eyes scanned the perimeter. They were smart enough to know a potential rouse when they saw one. Both men remained on high alert, but not high enough to realize the real threat was only a stride away.

"Now," Hadley said.

The guards' eyes went wide as the mystic dropped the magic that made he and Parker invisible. Landing a fist to one man's face, Hadley dropped his man before he could respond.

Parker wasn't quite as ready for it.

"The hell!" the other guard yelled as he reached out and grabbed Parker by the cloak.

Pushing his hands up between them, Parker shoved the guard, breaking his hold and slamming him against the door of the hut. Before the man could right himself, Parker swung the butt of his spear up, knocking the guard out cold.

"Why the hell didn't we just knock them out when we were invisible?" His eyes narrowed on Hadley.

"Hardly seems fair, does it?" Hadley gave him a grin and walked through the door.

The chief's hut was simple. Its open floor plan expanded from a general living space into a dining area where Sef stood behind the table, a set of bolas hanging from his side.

"What the hell is this all about?" He immediately reached for his weapon. "I've not used one of these since I was a younger man, but I still know how they work, you treacherous bastards. I never should have trusted you."

Even with his words drenched in scorn, the man's face, red and puffy, still looked more jolly than angry.

Parker slung his spear and held up his hands. "Cool it, boss. We're only here to help."

"Were you here to help them?" Sef nodded to the men unconscious on the other side of the doorway.

Parker shrugged. "Fair point. But really, just sit down—"

"I will do no such thing. I wanted to believe in you and the magician, but now I know the truth." He spun the bola by his side. Eyes narrowed, his kind demeanor all but gone. "I expect that I will not take you both, but before I am through, in the name of my son, I will take one of you bastards with me!"

Hadley held his right hand up toward the table, and his eyes flashed with the magic inside of him. An image appeared of Vatan, walking through her house.

"What the devil is this?" Sef spat.

"Let me show you more," Hadley said. "Then you can make your decision."

Keeping his hands high, Hadley crossed the room weaving around the table. Without asking for permission, he grabbed Sef's free hand. His eyes flashed again, and the chief shouted. Hadley, letting the man into his head, replayed the scene he had experienced earlier that night. He could hear her humming with glee.

"Vatan?" he whispered.

"It is," Hadley replied. "Now, this is what she is thinking."

An image came into Sef's mind, blurry at first. But in a second's time, it sharpened into a clear image of his son bound, a black arrow of Kofken lodged in his stomach, blood pouring from its entry point. Samet's face was drawn and white as a ghost. Then it turned into a picture of Sef, dead on the ground.

Sef gasped. "You monster, why are you doing this to me?"

Hadley let the image go. Taking one step back from the distraught father, he said, "I'm sorry. You need to see the truth. This is not some fantasy; I've never seen your son. It is all from her mind."

"But..." Sef mumbled. "So, he's gone?"

"No," Parker jumped into the conversation. "We don't think he is. Hadley believes this is just Vatan imagining what is *going* to happen. Don't worry, Hannah will save him."

"You bet your skinny Arcadian ass she will," a voice said from the doorway.

They all turned to see Hannah standing at the threshold, Dardanus behind her and Samet at her side.

"Father!" the boy shouted as he sped across the room and into Sef's big, beefy arms.

"My son, my son," the chief said, over and over again with

tears streaming down his chubby face. "I thought... I thought I might never see you again."

Hannah chimed in, "OK, what the hell is going on here? Why did I just see Karl running around the city with his ass hanging out?"

CHAPTER SEVENTEEN

They all sat around Sef's table and shared their stories, trying to piece together the tales of deceit. With only a small amount of protest, Gregory and Sal were left aboard the *Unlawful* and told to move it safely out of range. Ezekiel wanted to come meet the chief, but couldn't risk any more danger to the airship.

Hannah basically had to pull Laurel off of Gregory when they dropped down near the village.

Dardanus stood as he spoke, sharing all the details of their quest to find Samet, and the way in which their journey led them to the lookout shelter sitting over Kofken.

"We believed it was Kofken that decided to break the peace with us," he said, "but now that I know it was members of our own guard, I'm not sure what to think."

Sef shook his head. "Kofken may still have had a role to play in all of this, but I doubt it. Our true enemy was by my side this whole time."

Samet nodded. "It was Vatan. She wanted to draw as many guards away from the village as possible so she could kill my father without resistance. Then, with the village in an uproar over our deaths at the hands of Kofken assassins, she would be the strong leader that Baseek turned to."

Parker exhaled. "That hag is the worst. But I have to admit, it's a pretty solid plan—despite the sociopathic nature of it, I mean."

Sef nodded, his face was filled with concern. "Indeed. I let her get too close. Never saw that her lust for power was larger than I imagined. Being second wasn't enough. She was willing to kill us, to push us toward war for her own gain."

Ezekiel placed a hand on the man's shoulder. "Trust me, it can happen to the best of us."

The room grew quiet, filled with the gravity of a village betrayed by one they thought would sacrifice her life for them.

"Scheisse, you rock throwing, long-armed, imbecile sons of bitches, let me go!" the familiar gruff voice shouted from the doorway.

The group turned to see Karl, red in the face and panting from exhaustion, being pulled in by four of the Baseeki guards.

Hannah, not being able to hold it in, began to laugh good and hard. She felt the joy from Karl's annoyance rush through her. The rest of the room joined in.

His face grew brighter red. "Aye, yer sittin' here talkin' while I'm out doin' all the work." He turned to the chief. "Tell these bitches to get their bloody hands off a me."

Sef laughed and raised a hand. "Nice work, my men. But the rearick is our friend, and for all of life he will be. Let him go and fetch a bottle for him and one for the rest of us."

Karl straightened his cloak, pulling his leather vest down straight. He cast a dirty look at Parker. "Were you gonna tell him to call his dogs off or what?"

Grinning, Parker pointed at Karl's gut, pushing against the leather. "Thought you could use a mile or two under your belt today, Karl. Would be good for you after so many days on the airship."

The guards set a bottle and a glass in front of him. Skipping the glass, he put the bottle to his lips, tilting it and sucking in the ale as fast as it would come. After a good minute, he pulled it away, belched, and raised a middle finger to Parker. "Well, screw you and yer little work out, laddie."

They all laughed again as Karl turned for more of the bitter drink.

Finally, Samet spoke again. "Father, what about Vatan?"

"Indeed," he said, nodding to his son. Then he turned to Dardanus, who was just settling into the table. "Do not get comfortable. The work of the captain is never over." He pointed to the men that had brought Karl into his hut. "Take these men and go find the traitor. I imagine by now she is miles away, but I want her laying at my feet as soon as possible."

Dardanus smiled and nodded. "As always, I am at your service, sir." Turning to Aysa, he said, "Think you have one more adventure in you tonight?"

Aysa gasped. "Do you mean it?"

"I sure do. You've proven yourself a fine warrior and a shrewd judge. I could use your help." Dardanus left with Aysa by his side and the men behind them.

Sef then called for a porter from another room. The man stood in the doorway, waiting for his orders. "My son was gone, now he has returned. Wake the town and prepare the beach for the kutlam. We will celebrate until the sun arrives and sets again!"

"Kutlam?" Hannah asked.

Samet looked at her, confusion on his face. "You don't have kutlam?"

She laughed. "Sounds like a disease."

The boy smiled, which she hadn't yet seen from him. "The furthest from a sickness. It's the word we reserve for a party... a party of the highest order. You'll love it!"

Sef turned to Hadley. "Your powers are impressive, mystic.

I'm wondering if, while the kutlam is prepared, you would flatter me with one more task."

Hadley stood and bowed to the chief. "It is an honor to serve at your pleasure, sir."

Karl belched and laughed. "Careful, pretty boy. Never know what this one wants when he's feelin' festive."

Ignoring the rearick, Sef said, "Good. Come with me. The rest of you can take your time to rest and clean up. We have a long night ahead of us!"

Sef left with Hadley at his hip. Hannah looked around the room at her friends back together again and couldn't stop smiling.

Hannah stared at the ceiling, flat on her back, in the little room that Sef had given her for the night. The Baseek community outside the hut was electric with excitement for the village-wide party that was about to happen down on the beach, and she was just happy to have a few minutes alone to close her eyes and regain her strength.

It had been a hell of a few days, and, although they had only wanted to take a stop to stretch their legs, the fact they had made a difference for a little out of the way village made her happy. It made her wonder how many calamities they had passed over since their departure from Arcadia.

She thought about Ezekiel and his failed attempts to connect with Lilith. While she had no idea what the entire mission was really about, she trusted him that it was necessary. And, in times like these, she imagined that their work might usher in a time of global peace—a world-wide kutlam, which might carry on forever.

The door squeaked as it opened, and Hannah jumped, the dagger that Karl had given her a lifetime ago, at the ready.

She relaxed as she saw the gentle eyes of Parker staring through the crack in the door.

"Am I interrupting anything?" he asked.

"Yes, you son of a bitch! Get the hell out of here."

He nodded, then slowly backed away.

"I'm shitting you," Hannah said, scooting across the bed toward the stone wall. She patted the empty space next to her. "Come join me."

Parker looked down at his feet and then back at her. He pulled the door closed behind him and crossed the room, easing himself into the empty spot on the bed. He laid his head on a pillow, his nose inches from hers.

"Welcome," she said with a smile. "Hopefully your mom doesn't know you're here."

"She always liked you." Parker smiled. "Even though you were a bad influence on me."

Hannah's mind wandered back to their life before Ezekiel. It was easy to divide life that way. BE and AE, that was the way she considered things. "I'm sure that's how she saw it."

He laughed. "Probably. She'd be shocked to know it was actually the other way around." He paused for a moment, and they just looked into each other's eyes, neither of them blinking. "I'm glad you're back," he said, finally breaking the comfortable silence.

"Me, too," she said. "I much prefer to kick ass with you by my side. Then I know I can always save your butt if you need me to."

He laughed, though he knew she was telling the truth. "We had it easy. I mostly just sat in a jail cell and watched Karl get shitfaced. Felt kind of bad with you out there risking your neck with a bunch of long arms."

Hannah smiled and nestled her head further into her pillow. "It was nothing. And this new girl, Aysa..."

"Oh, you have a little crush?"

"Maybe. She's pretty damned cool. Reminds me of us when

we were out there hustling. Lost her parents a few years back, and now she doesn't fit in anywhere."

Parker laughed. "Sounds like our kind of girl."

"Yeah." She smiled and closed her eyes, an image of Gregory and Laurel on the deck came to mind, causing her to laugh.

"What?"

"Nothing," Hannah said. "Just thinking of..." She trailed off.

"Thinking of what?"

"I wish you were there. When we got back to the ship, Laurel and Gregory, they..."

"Yeah?"

"As soon as boots were on the deck, those two were sucking face like their lives depended on it." She giggled.

"Sounds nice," Parker said.

Hannah's eyes snapped open, a grin on Parker's face met her. "Is that right?" she asked.

"It's very right. I mean, they've known it was coming for a while. They weren't stupid, after all."

"Yeah," Hannah whispered. "Because it would be altogether stupid for two people to know they want it and to hold themselves back, right?"

"That is *so* right," he said.

She froze, waiting for Parker to make the move, but he was like a statue.

Screw it, she thought as she leaned in and planted her lips on his.

He melted immediately, like he had been waiting for this for years. She felt his warm tongue against hers. They kissed, just like that, for what felt like a lifetime.

But it couldn't last forever.

The noise from the party outside grew louder, and Hannah pulled away. "We'll, um, be expected at the beach."

Parker laughed. "Like you've ever done what's expected of you."

He pulled her in, and they kissed for another lifetime.

Torches laced the night sky, competing with the full moon overhead as Hannah and Parker walked down to the shoreline, hand in hand. Her heart raced, faster than in any battle against an enemy. Her eyes traced the waves on the water.

"I've never seen it before, you know," she said.

"The ocean? Me neither. It goes on forever."

"At least as far as we can see. It's like magic. I can't see where it ends, but it's gotta have its own limits."

Parker squeezed her hand as they stumbled together down the rocky path. "Why do you assume that there is a limit to your magic?"

Hannah shrugged. "Dunno. I guess everything has limits."

"I doubt we'll ever find yours," he responded, his eyes locked on the water that stretched out toward the horizon.

With no response, she kept her eyes on the lapping waves. Spending all of her life in Arcadia, and most of it within the Boulevard, her world was pretty small. But knowing how much distance they had travelled, and how much more they had to go, Hannah couldn't help but marvel at just how big their world was.

She and Parker wove their way through the reveling crowd. The Baseeki were ecstatic: feasting, drinking, dancing together under the moon. She stopped and watched Karl, stripped to the waist and circling a large Baseeki warrior while a crowd cheered on.

"What do you think?" Parker asked her. "That Baseeki is probably twice his size."

Hannah smiled. "I didn't bet against you when you fought a man twice your size in the Pit. And I sure as hell wouldn't bet against Karl."

They moved on, finally finding their crew. They sat on seats carved out of logs surrounding a fire, feet away from the ocean. Aysa and Dardanus were a part of the circle.

"Where have you two been?" Laurel asked as they let go of each other's hands and joined their friends.

"Just resting... I mean, well, I was resting, and so was Parker." Hannah felt herself blush, and she hoped the moonlight wouldn't betray her.

"So, that's what you call it?" Laurel cooed.

They all laughed and let Parker and Hannah settle into the remaining seats. A small fire burned in the middle as the party raged around them. Ezekiel sat across the circle from her, happily puffing on his pipe.

Hannah looked over at Dardanus. "So, you found her?"

"Vatan?" he asked, his eyes on the fire. "No. She isn't in Baseek, that's for sure. It didn't take long for me and my men to search the place. She's gone now. But your man did his job."

Hannah glanced over at Hadley, who pushed his hand through his hair. "Is that right?" she asked.

"I have a way of sniffing out the enemy," he said with a grin. "Found nearly a dozen of those bastards who worked with her. I doubt it will take much time to find her, but on her own, she won't do much damage anyway. We've cut the snakes legs off."

"Um," Laurel said, "you know snakes don't have legs, right?"

"OK," Hadley sighed. "Bad metaphor. Anyway, she doesn't have anybody now. I think all will be safe in Baseek."

Dardanus cleared his throat. "We will find her. You don't have to worry about that, and Sef is going with full guard day after tomorrow to Kofken. We still assume that Vatan was working on her own, trying to vilify Kofken so she could gain power, but better safe than sorry."

Karl ambled over to the crew, shirt still in hand.

"That didn't take long," Hannah chirped.

"Eh, dat one was an OK fighter. Almost felt badly for him," Karl snorted. "Well, when ya find that Vatan, give her hell fer me.

I got a few broken ribs that are just screamin' for payback. Now, fer once in my life, I'm sick of all this war talk. Can we drink and laugh for a while? *Scheisse*, we bloody won!"

Hannah raised her glass. "I'll drink to that!"

They all cried, "Here, here!" and clinked their glasses, drinking down the Baseeki brew.

Ezekiel stood, raising his mug toward the heavens. "Friends, I am glad you got a chance to stretch your legs, though I never thought it would result in this kind of adventure. But I have no disappointment. Our friend Marcus, who stayed back in our fair city, once said, 'Any injustice is an injustice worth righting.' And I agree with him. So, tonight, we rejoice for Baseek. But tomorrow, we continue on, for we need to make it to the Oracle. She holds—"

A sound like thunder interrupted Ezekiel's speech, and it rolled on as if it would go forever. The magician looked over to Laurel, but the druid shook her head. It was no natural disruption, but something altogether different. He narrowed his eyes and turned his gaze toward the grassy slope that fell toward the sea.

"We're not alone!" Ezekiel screamed into the night air.

Hannah looked up to see hundreds of torches lighting the night sky. Drums beat on without rhythm or order, filling the air with noise.

"Roamers," Dardanus said through a clenched jaw.

"There's hundreds of them," Karl snorted.

"Well, hundreds of torches at least." Hannah eyes glowed red in the excitement. "This is going to be fun!"

Aysa jumped to her feet. "What's a party without a little bloodshed?"

The sound of hooves rumbled from above as the roaming men descended.

"To arms!" Sef screamed over the roar.

Men and women alike, sprang into action. Most of them spun

bolas by their sides, waiting for the warriors they could hear to come into sight. Others were already launching rocks blindly in the direction of the approaching forces. Older ladies scooped up the youngest children and ran for shelter.

The sound of approaching horses stopped, and the night air became dead quiet.

"The hell are they doing?" Parker whispered.

"Aye, maybe they saw me hammer and thought better of a fight," Karl responded, his eyes squinting into the darkness.

The silence broke with the whistling sound of arrows, scores of them, piercing the night air.

"Zeke, you take the right side," Hannah yelled, already throwing her arms toward the sky in an attempt to block the volley.

A few got through the seam between her shield and Ezekiel's, several finding their targets in the Baseeki fighters ahead of them. Hannah shifted as the next round came, overlapping their cover.

"They won't be able to hold that for long!" Hadley yelled. "And if we can't take out the archers, we're screwed."

"I got this," Laurel said. As she ran in the direction of the attackers.

Laurel moved through the darkness, toward the sound of hooves.

She narrowed her gaze at the man leading the charge. Armor bouncing with the horse's rhythm, his eyes were filled with violence. A smile split across his face when the young druid came into view. Raising a club hewn from the bone of something truly massive, he let out a war-cry.

But Laurel didn't move. She held her ground, calm as a summer morning. Her apparent boredom drove him to ride faster.

And still, she didn't move.

Hannah yelled as the horse flew toward her, about to trample her into the sand. But at the last moment, the druid twisted, side-stepping the horse on the opposite side of the roamer's attacking hand. She reached up and grabbed the man's cloak, pulling herself onto the horse's back behind him.

"Yeah, I'm gonna need your ride," she said as she jerked the guy off the steed.

With her hands on the bridle, she whispered a word into the horse's ear and pulled it off its main course. Kicking her heels, she pushed the steed toward her group.

"You! Get on!" she yelled at Parker. He pulled himself up behind her and draped an arm around her waist. "Gonna take a stronger hold than that!" she shouted over her shoulder before turning the horse back into action.

They charged toward the archers, Laurel guiding the horse through the oncoming horde of attackers. The creature danced with every flick of her wrist on the bridle, as if their minds were connected and working as one.

Parker held tight with his left arm and swung his spear with his right, dropping anyone who got close enough. As the crowd thinned and the oncoming men fled from the path of the horse and its ass-kicking passengers, Parker flipped the spear and steadied it under his arm so he could send blasts of magitech energy into the scurrying crowd.

"Suck it, bitches!" he shouted as he volleyed beams of light at anyone he could find.

"Nice work!" Laurel shouted. "Now, keep your head down."

"What do you—" Parker didn't need to complete the question. Looking over the druid's shoulder, he saw they were getting close to the archers, but they had turned their bows from the sky to them. "Ah, shit!"

Laurel could hear the commander's call, as they all let loose their arrows at once. "You've got this," she said to the horse between her legs and dropped the reins.

Her trust in the animal was not misplaced. The war horse cut and weaved, somehow finding a path through the wall of arrows. Five feet from the archers, Laurel screamed to Parker, "He's all yours!" She gave the animal a swift kick before she dove off of its back. Parker shouted as the steed ran into the darkness.

Hitting the ground, Laurel rolled onto her feet, crouching with her blade in hand. The captain of the archers only had a second to grasp what was about to happen to him.

Laurel spun the blade, then launched it toward him. He grabbed his bleeding throat and fell to the ground.

Wasting no time, Laurel spun, pulling the blade with her and took out two more men. The archers figured out what was happening and exchanged their bows for blades.

Laurel pulled a second dagger from her hip, ready for close quarter combat. "Need some help here!" she shouted. Devin crawled up out of the folds of her cloak onto her shoulder. "Sorry, buddy." She grinned as she threw her secret weapon toward one of the archers.

Devin responded perfectly, biting and clawing at the man's eyes until he ran for his life. The squirrel dropped to the ground and bounded toward her next victim, who tried to swipe the squirrel away with his longbow. Laurel laughed as her friend hopped left and then scurried up the man's leather clothing.

"Laugh at this, bitch," a voice shouted from behind her.

Spinning, Laurel stared down the head of an arrow ready to launch.

The archer loosed it, and Laurel dodged, the projectile sinking deep into the gut of a man behind her.

"Who's the bitch now?" She took three quick strides then jumped, landing on his chest. He was dead before they hit the ground.

A hand grabbed her ponytail and pulled. "You're gonna pay for that," he said, raising his sword.

Her only response was to smile, as she saw blue light reflected off the man's blade. A half second later, the blast from Parker's staff leveled him.

"Let's go," he said, pulling her up onto the horse's back in front of him. "I think you've sown enough chaos here. But you'd better drive—I hate these things."

"Thanks," Laurel said before ticking her tongue against her teeth.

Devin hopped off a man's fallen body and ran for them, jumping up into Laurel's arms. "Good girl," she said as the bloody squirrel squirmed into the folds of her cloak.

"That thing is freaky scary. Someday, you're gonna have to tell me how she got her name."

Laurel scowled as she pulled on the reins, turning the horse downhill where the fighting was heating up.

'Over my dead body!"

CHAPTER EIGHTEEN

"Come on, I ain't even broken a bloody sweat yet!" Karl shouted as he bowled over men and women, one after another.

His war hammer was a terror, and the short blades and clubs of the roamers were no match for it. He kept pushing through the crowd, leaving a wake of broken bodies in his path. Leveling two more men, he broke into an open space by the edge of the sea. Taking a deep breath, he looked for his next victim.

"Damn," a voice said from his right. "I didn't know the Baseeki came in fun size."

Karl turned to see a man larger than any of the others walking toward him. The moonlight caught his sword shaped from a human bone. It was dirtied with the blood of the Baseeki fighters he had killed.

"Step a little closer, and I'll show ya how fun I can be."

The man laughed, but he began circling. "You know, my father once told me a story about short men like you from the east. He said he knew a man to kill a hundred fighters without pause, only to pick up his hammer and kill another hundred more. Are you that man? Because I've always wanted to try my luck against him."

Karl laughed, moving to the right so as to keep his distance. "Not yet." He glanced over his shoulder. "Think I have ten or twelve to go." He gripped his hammer in his right hand. "Ya wanna be next?"

The man sneered. "Not until you tell me your name."

"Aye, the hell ya askin' for?"

"I collect the names of the men I kill, when I can at least. It's nice to know who I wipe off the face of Irth. It's my offering to the old gods."

Karl snorted. "Then ya won't be needin' mine, ya half-wit son of a twat." He grit his teeth and then yelled, "Let's do this!"

With a scream, he rushed the man, hammer swinging down from over his head as he went. Karl's opponent swiped it away with his bonesword, and dodged to the right.

Karl laughed. "Finally, somebody worth fightin'. Most of you roamers have shit for brains and piss for talent."

This time, the man attacked, swinging the sword for Karl's head. Ducking, he stepped in and drove the butt of his hammer into the man's gut and then snapped it up, knocking the man's head back.

He wiped a line of blood from his lip and smiled. "Oh, yes. I'm going to enjoy this."

"Good," Karl spat. "It'll be the last thing ye enjoy."

He drove his sword at Karl too quickly for the rearick to respond. The tip of his blade found the crease between his leathers, biting at his left arm.

"Scheisse!" Karl yelled.

"Your name, sir? I'll make this quicker."

"Screw you!"

The man drove again, but this time, Karl was ready for him. Instead of ducking, he swung his hammer to meet the attack. It shattered the blade into a thousand pieces. Karl dropped his hammer, grabbed the man's hand and shoved the broken blade backward into the man's soft belly.

The roamer's eyes grew wide as Karl twisted the hilt.

"The name's Karl, ya filthy bastard. When ya get to hell, you can tell 'em who sent ya."

Karl pulled the blade up, slicing through the man's chest. He watched as his foe dropped to the ground, blood spilling all around him.

Hannah blasted a group of attackers back and into the cold, dark waters surrounding them. Eyes flashing red, she pointed her finger at the sea and it froze it over, covering the enemy in an icy grave.

She turned, looking for the next person to fight. But for the first time, she was alone on the beach. "Damn," she said as she took a second to watch the battle raging around her. The rocky ground was covered with bodies, roamers and Baseeki alike. Her eyes caught movement up the shore.

"Samet!" she shouted as she ran toward Sef's son, wondering what the hell he was doing out in the melee. He held a bola meekly in his hand, but he looked scared shitless by the battle. He was too distraught to notice the tall, dark figure approaching him from behind.

Focusing her energy as she sprinted on the soft sand, Hannah raised her hand toward the attacker, but before she could fire, a shocking pain penetrated her leg, dropping her to the ground. "Queen Bitch!" she yelled, finding a roamer's arrow lodged in her quad. Gritting her teeth, she tried to ignore it and turned for the boy.

In the light of the moon, she saw his assailant. "Vatan, no!"

The evil woman must have used the chaos of the fight to sneak close to her prey. Even though the whole village now knew of her treachery, it seemed she was still intent on drawing blood.

Hannah limped as fast as she could, but it was too slow. Vatan grabbed Samet, threw him to the ground, and raised a wicked knife.

But before the woman could land her deadly blow, a rock came out of nowhere, crashing into her hand. The knife fell, and in a flash, Aysa was on top of her, landing punch after punch with her one arm on the woman's face.

By the time Hannah reached her, Vatan, the traitor, was dead.

"I saved you," Aysa said to Samet, who lay quivering next to her. "Holy shit, that was awesome."

A man came out of nowhere, tackling Aysa off of Vatan's lifeless body. He pinned her down, hate and rage dripping from his lips. 'You're too pretty to be out here now. Looks like I'll have to teach you a lesson," he said with a yellow glint in his eye. "Should be fun."

Aysa turned to Samet. "Help me!"

The boy looked at her wide-eyed. He shook his head, only a little, got up, and ran off into the darkness.

"You're not having any fun tonight," Hannah grunted as she pulled the arrow from her leg and drove it through the man's throat.

'Thank you," Aysa wheezed, pushing the body off of her. "I can't believe he…" She looked off in the direction that her friend had run.

Hannah reached down and pulled Aysa to her feet. "Don't worry. You don't need him to protect you. Not when we girls stick together."

"You bet your ass we will," Aysa said, a smile creeping onto her face. "I thought I loved him. But did you see that dickweed run?"

"Hell yeah!" Hannah yelled. She looked up toward the battle and saw the marauders gaining ground, pushing the Baseeki and her crew back toward the water. "Come on. Let's go end this!"

Hadley stood between Karl and Ezekiel, watching the roamers advance. The mystic did what he could, warning his friends of danger. But he wasn't a fighter—not like the two old men next to him. Karl spun like a wild man—his hammer a blur of metal and death. Zeke took down scores at a time with fire and light and illusion. But the roamers kept attacking, undeterred by the prodigious display of force.

"They got us pinned," Karl grumbled as he smashed a roamer's head in. "Too many of the damned bastards, even if they fight like children. Ya knock one down and three more are on ya."

"Agreed," Ezekiel said. "I guess it's time to bring in the heavy guns. Hadley, see if you can buy me some time."

The mystic nodded. "Not a problem!"

Hadley crossed his arms. His face turned as expressionless as the cliffs that surrounded them, and his eyes clouded over with white.

"Bloody magicians," Karl grumbled.

No sooner did the words cross his lips then the sand between them and the charging army started to shift before his eyes. Out of the ground rose a giant mass of dirt that twisted and turned as it grew. The sand morphed into a creature nearly twenty feet tall. It raised its hands over its massive head and roared into the dead night air. Slamming the ground, it sent tremors through them all.

The roamers stopped in their tracks, in awe of the monster rising to attack them. They were content to fight Baseeki warriors and outlandish magicians, but the creature was where they drew the line. Most turned to flee for the hills that stood above them, screaming in terror, but several brave warriors, hoping to buy some time, went on the offensive. Drawing their longbows, they shot wildly at the creature, their arrows flying right through and out the other side.

"Wait!" they screamed. "It isn't real. Damned thing is a trick."

A few more tested that theory, launching rocks and arrows at it. Slowly, the roamers reformed their ranks and returned to the beach to continue their onslaught.

"Shit," Hadley yelled. "That didn't take very long."

"Must be losin' yer touch," Karl replied. As he spoke, a great wind rose up behind him.

"It held them back long enough," Ezekiel shouted over the noise. The old man stood ankle deep in the sea as a great storm swirled up around him. Lightning flashed all around, and Karl could see the eyes of the roamers, who readied themselves for their final push.

"Come on wizard," he snorted. "Enough with the light show. Strike 'em dead already."

"Patience, Karl."

Hannah sprinted down the shoreline with Aysa close on her heels. "Shit," she said, coming to Hadley's side. "Pretty good one."

"Too bad they've found me out," the mystic said, eyes still covered in white.

A roamer charged toward Hannah, but before she got a chance to use her knife, a spear burst through his chest. Parker and Laurel jumped off the horse and joined their companions.

Looking at the storm, and the few Baseeki still in fighting condition, Parker shouted, "I'm glad the big man's on our side, but I don't think his storm is gonna be enough to stop 'em. Ezekiel's powerful, but this army seems endless. We don't have enough men."

Karl laughed as his hammer knocked a roamer's leg clean off. "Thanks fer the pep talk kid, but I don't exactly see a plan B here. We're givin' 'em everything we've got."

Hannah opened her mouth to respond, but a loud voice caught her attention. She turned toward the roamers and saw a man standing in front of them—his face swollen to hell.

"Hello, witch!" Altan shouted. "I'm here for your airship. It's gonna make our business run a lot smoother. But I'm glad I get to

197

kill along the way. I think we'll stick your body on the front as a warning to those who oppose us."

Hannah glared at the man, cursing herself for her act of mercy. Cal was right, the roamers couldn't be trusted.

But Hannah was happy for a chance to make good on her promise.

She looked across at her friends, fighting side by side to save a people that weren't their own. She was worried for their safety, sick of the needless destruction raining down around them. But most of all, she felt a burning in her chest, a desire to make the world better, to wipe scum like this man off the face of the earth.

It was a feeling she hadn't had since the day Sal came into her world.

She turned to Parker. "We haven't given them everything... yet. I think we've been holding back."

Parker smiled. "So, what's the plan."

"Let go."

Hannah closed her eyes and reached out to Hadley. Despite the chaos of the fight, she could hear his thoughts crystal clear.

What do you need? he thought.

I'm going to try something crazy, she replied. *I need you to keep up that illusion for as long as you can.*

Sure, but they know it's fake. What are you going to do?

A wicked smile crossed her lips as she thought, *Show them they're wrong.*

Hannah opened her eyes. They blazed with a red fury. She held a palm parallel to the ground, then made a fist. Sand and rock and driftwood leapt at her command. She focused on Hadley's mirage, while twisting her hands in a rapid pattern. All the elements that she raised from the ground poured into the creature, filling the work of his imagination with actual fragments of the earth.

"Hold it," she uttered to Hadley. Her concentration was

intense, and she felt like the power inside of her was about to break through her skin.

She turned to Laurel. "It needs life. Can you help?"

The druid looked in confusion, then suddenly began to understand the plan. She planted her hands in the sand, and as her eyes flashed green, roots from deep under the earth grew, wrapping around the imaginary monster.

"Uh, Hannah," Parker shouted as he fired his spear rapidly into the oncoming crowd. "I don't mean to interrupt playtime, but what the hell are you doing?"

"You'll see," she said, a wicked smile again creeping across her face. She turned and looked at Ezekiel, whose expression was a mixture of shock and pride. He nodded, and she reached her hand toward him.

The storm responded.

A bolt of lightning broke through the heavens. She clenched her jaw as it crashed into her; the heat and pain almost too much to bear. But she held on, and with a strength she didn't know she had, she turned and directed the power back out. It sprung from her outstretched palm, connecting with the hodgepodge of sand and root and mental energy in front of her. The power from the lightning fused the mess together.

Hannah screamed—and the creature responded.

It roared, it's cavernous voice echoing across the beach.

The roamers took a step back, before Altan shouted. "Don't be fooled by that whore's tricks. You can run right through it! Slaughter them all."

The creature turned to look at Hannah, and she nodded in reply. "Go get 'em."

The thing raised a leg high into the air.

"It's a trick!" Altan shouted, his voice dripping with arrogance as the creature's foot hovered over him. "It's only a—"

The foot dropped to the ground, crushing Altan like a bug.

The roamers fell backward in awe.

Hannah turned and looked at the people around her. "Now, we have the help we need. Let's gut these fuckers!"

The creature ran forward, stomping roamers beneath its heels. The remaining Baseeki army followed behind it, shrieking in joy as they cut through anyone dumb enough to stand in their way.

It was a righteous slaughter.

Some roamers kept their heads and struck back at the creature. Each hit broke off a piece of its body, but not nearly enough to slow it down.

A particularly brave roamer climbed onto the thing's back. But it reached back and plucked the man from his shoulders, as if he were a gnat. The monster launched the man into a mass of his friends, knocking them down like they were weeds.

Hannah smiled as she sank to the ground. The image of the creature she had brought to life faded as her world began to swim.

Parker fell to his knees beside her, holding her upright with his arm. "Don't worry. I've got you."

Karl dropped his hammer, his mouth gaping and his eyes fixed on the ugly giant destroying the enemy. "What the bloody hell is that thing?"

Hannah glanced up at him, the red glow slowly fading from her eyes. "Not sure. But it sure as shit is kicking ass!"

She laughed, then promptly passed out.

EPILOGUE

The hum of the magitech core filled their ears. Hannah sat at the head of the long table in the captain's cabin that Gregory had transformed into their headquarters. She could hardly keep the smile from her face as she watched each of the members of her crew file in, one by one.

Faces were drawn, and eyes were dark with exhaustion, but she didn't care. All of the members were weary with the fatigue that only working for a better world could provide. Karl walked in, giving a heave and humph as he landed solidly in his chair. The only one missing was Ezekiel.

Karl glanced out the porthole toward the sun, which careened toward the horizon. "Scheisse, wizard! Always late."

Hadley jabbed him with an elbow. "Looked like the magicians used all their discipline saving your hammer-swinging ass last night, little man."

"Screw you," Karl replied with a grin. "If that stuffed animal didn't get in my way, I woulda finished 'em all off myself. Damn wizards, every one of ya!"

They all laughed, until Parker said, "Don't include me in their ranks."

He swatted his hand at Parker. "Nah, yer good, kid. Though one of these days, I'll get ya to use a proper spear that don't need them magic rocks. Kinda cheatin' if ya ask me."

"Yeah," Hannah said. "He didn't. But I'm asking something, what the hell happened last night anyway, I mean, after I dropped on the beach?"

Everyone at the table started to tell the tale at once, each accentuating their own heroics. Finally, stopping them, she turned to Parker. "Just you," she said.

Laurel snickered. "Now that you two are sucking face, you're going to play favorites."

Hannah flushed, "We didn't suck—"

"Yeah," Parker interrupted her. "In case you forgot, we did have an intimate moment before going down to the party."

"Of course, I—"

He held up his hand. "It's OK. My ego is strong. Let's skip to the end of the battle."

Parker recounted how the monster that she and the other magicians had made together, each focusing on their own specialty, brought hell on Irth to the roamers until Hannah had run out of power and dropped to the sand, nearly unconscious.

Thanks to the brilliant combination, the enemy was all but defeated. Many ran for their lives, but were overtaken quickly by the Baseeki warriors, thirsty for victory for their place over an enemy who had no home. Any who stayed to fight didn't last long as Hannah's crew struck down the remainder.

"Glad you finished them," Hannah smiled. "I felt like I ran to Arcadia and back after thirty seconds of holding that beast together."

"Surprised you did it for that long," Hadley quipped. "It was one badass casting."

Gregory laughed nervously. "Glad I missed it."

"Aye," Karl snorted. "Thing was a monster. I still might have a little shit in me britches."

They all laughed, while Hannah smiled and nodded her thanks. After the fight, the Baseeki people put them up for the night in their finest huts, taking time to tend to their wounds. Karl's arm was still sore, where a sword bit his flesh. In his stubbornness, Karl refused magical healing.

"We rearick," he had said, "fix ourselves... the old-fashioned way!"

Most of them slept half the following day away, and it wasn't until Ezekiel insisted on the urgency of their mission that most of them walked back to the *Unlawful*—the old magician teleporting himself and his still-comatose student back to her chambers.

Just as Parker was finishing the story, Ezekiel stepped through the doorway and into their new headquarters. The old man smiled, turned to Hannah, and said, "Looks like we're ready to begin, Captain."

She felt a flush fall over her. For a year she had followed his lead—though it had felt like it had been a lifetime—and now, he was ushering the eyes of the membership toward her. She still wasn't sure why he would do such a thing.

They all turned toward her, and she hesitated.

Karl broke the uncomfortable silence hanging in the room. "Scheisse, it was good to stretch me damned legs, but I, for one, am ready to get this bucket of bolts moving toward our final destination. Whatta ya say, kid?" He nodded at Gregory.

Hannah could feel him shift at her side. The engineer took the rearick's comment for a command and moved to comply, but he settled back in when Hannah placed a gentle hand on his forearm. With a nod, she affirmed his presence in the room.

Getting used to her command would still take some time for all of them, especially for Hannah herself, but the shift in perspective from Ezekiel's leadership to Hannah's was a necessary one, particularly for what lay ahead on their journey to save Irth.

"Thanks, Zeke. But now, as you turn the command over to me, I want to turn the floor back to you." She raised a brow to her mentor, and he raised one in reply. "Up until now, you have done well to gather us, train us, and even let us know that we are on some greater journey. I mean, the Bitch and the Bastard know we were all so damned surprised when you told us you hadn't come back to Arcadia to defeat Adrien, but to assemble a team. I'd call that a big-ass pile of bricks you landed on us all."

The old magician's eyes sparkled, and the corners of his mouth turned up in a smile. "Indeed. I expect it was."

"Right then," she said. "Before I send my engineer to the cockpit, before I send any of my people one foot further toward the mission in your mind, I declare it is time for you to spill the freaking beans. What the hell are we doing out here?" She passed him a smile.

Ezekiel pulled his bowl from his bag and started to pack it with some of the local Baseeki weed he had purchased off of one of the locals below. His hands moved deftly with the habit formed by a lifetime of the movements; his eyes never broke his gaze on his student, who was now his leader. Raising the stem to his lips, his eyes sparked a light red, and a flame rose off his fingertip.

After a few long draws, he returned her smile through a long smoky exhale. "Seems you've had no problem assuming the mantel of leadership."

"Yeah, I know I'm still the new girl," Laurel said, "but I'm preeeetty sure she can do anything."

Hannah glanced at Laurel and then over to Gregory. "Still working on dancing, but that's another story. Let's hear it, Zeke."

The old wizard leaned back in his chair and threw his boots up on the table, crossing his legs at the ankle. "OK, it's storytime. I told all of you that the Oracle, Lilith, was a being of great power. But she's been locked in combat with a being whose strength surpasses her own for the last forty years. It's why I left

Arcadia years ago, leaving the place in the hands of Adrien—my first student, whom I trusted."

'We saw how that worked out," Karl grunted, his cheeks turning red from the ale.

"Yes, Karl. He wasn't ready for the power. Maybe he never would have been." Ezekiel placed his feet back on the floorboards and drew from his own mug. "But I had no other choice. She needed me, and frankly, whether you want to hear it or not, Lilith's welfare was more important than the common good of just one city—even the city I had built with my own hands.

"And it's why I returned—because my help wasn't enough. An army of darkness like Irth has never known threatens to invade our world from another, violent creatures who want nothing more than to consume and destroy. We have a chance— a small one, mind you, but a chance nonetheless—to keep them out of Irth forever, stopping the war before it ever really begins."

Silence blanketed the room. Even Hannah was at a loss for words. She had gotten pieces of the puzzle from him for nearly a year but now the full picture was coming into view, and she didn't expect it to have anything to do with soldiers from another world.

Hannah sighed in relief when Parker finally said, "Shit, Ezekiel. With all due respect, don't you think this is something you should have told us earlier?"

Ezekiel looked out the western porthole, his eyes finding the gentle, moonlit waters below. With the slightest nod, he said, "I was hoping you could enjoy a trace of peace now, before we arrived at our destination. Because once we get there, we'll be fighting tooth and nail every step of the way."

Karl slammed his fist on the table, shaking the mugs of ale. 'Praise the mountains! I'm tired of all this sittin' around shite. If there's a war to fight, then ya can count on me to be on the front lines."

Everyone's heads nodded. Hannah spoke up, "And you can count on all of us to be right by your side."

The gravity of their situation sunk in. Each member of the team had a million questions, but none of them yet dared to ask them. A noise from behind an old crate, which belonged to the previous captain, grabbed their attention.

Like a sober man, ten years younger, Karl was on his feet and across the room. His arm shot into the shadows, and he pulled out a hooded figure, holding them by the folds of their robes, the hood dropped back exposing Aysa, face twisted up and glaring at the rearick.

Karl laughed. "Look what I caught. It's kind of scrawny, I say we throw it back."

Aysa balled her only hand into a tight fist and swung her long arm at Karl's head, connecting with his chin.

"Scheisse, girl!" he yelled, dropping her to the floor.

Getting up, Aysa dusted herself off. "Look who's talking, *tiny*." Then she turned toward Hannah's crew. "So, you're heading off to fight a dark, demon army from another world. I thought maybe you could use another set of hands." She raised her one arm. "Hand, really. But it's strong as hell. Tell 'em, Karl."

Hannah felt goosebumps rise on the back of her neck as she stood on the deck of the *Unlawful*. Though she wasn't sure if it was the feeling of the late spring air cutting through her hair or Parker's hand that was caressing her back beneath her shirt. Either way, she was happy, even knowing they were racing toward certain death.

It didn't take long for the crew to agree that Aysa should come with them. She fought with the spirit of an Arcadian rebel and added some fire power from a distance with her perfect aim with a rock. Even Karl, with a bruise on his chin beneath his beard, agreed. The girl was right, they were going to need all the help they could get against the army of darkness that Ezekiel had spoken of.

She craned her neck to watch the land below cruise past. "We should have brought the others," she said, almost inaudibly.

"What's that?" Parker smiled.

"Amelia, Julianne, Marcus… All of them. I'd feel better if they were here with us."

He nodded. "I know. But your tight ass is going to lead us to victory. I have no doubt about that." She slapped him lightly across the chest. "Besides, they're needed in Arcadia and in the Heights. It's a time of instability."

She nodded, but kept quiet for a moment. Parker was smart. Smarter than anyone she knew. Finally, she whispered, "You should be leading."

He laughed hard enough to bend at the waist. "Like hell, I should. Hey, I'll be your number two any day. You've got this."

Hannah tilted her head and leaned in toward him, longing to feel the warmth of his lips on hers.

"Run for cover!" a voice shouted, interrupting their moment.

Hannah's eyes shot open and found Gregory sprinting across the deck, his arms flailing wildly overhead.

"What is it?" she screamed as her hand reached for the hilt of her dagger at her hip.

"He… he… he…" Gregory sprinted. "I warned her, but she wouldn't freaking listen!"

Behind him, the door leading to the interior of the ship shattered, sending splinters of wood in every direction. Sal leaped out, tongue hanging out the side of his mouth, beady black eyes darting in every direction. He rushed wildly across the deck, sending the crew diving in every direction.

A beat after Sal burst through the door, Laurel crept out with an evil little smile on her face.

"Dammit, Laurel!" Hannah yelled across the deck. "You gave

my dragon your kaffe." Her voice sounded angry, but she couldn't hold back the smile.

Laurel shrugged. "He saved Gregory's life. I thought he deserved a little something special."

Sal took to the air, flying erratically, swooping in every direction.

Gregory hit the ground as the scaly beast almost knocked him over the rails. "Next time," he screamed at Laurel, "don't reward Sal for saving my life with something that might make him end it!"

The whole crew laughed on the deck as they dodged the hopped-up dragon.

Hannah drew Parker in close. "With this crew, I think we're going to do just fine."

Parker didn't respond, he just leaned in and gave her the kiss of her lifetime.

UNTITLED

Arcadians
(Artwork by Eric Quigley)

UNTITLED

Mystic
(Artwork by Eric Quigley)

Ok, this may seem weird, but the times I feel most like Hannah are when I finish writing a book. I've mentioned before that I'm nothing like our badass heroine. She's bold at the exact times when I'd be quaking in my boots. She's strong in places where my weakness shines through. She's sassy when I would be silent.

And I would NEVER call somebody a douche nugget. At least not to their face.

Maybe Chris.

But finishing up a book (if you'll pardon the self-aggrandizement) is like an explosion of magic that you didn't know you had in you. Hannah didn't know she could pull in everyone's talents to create that monster on the beach, but it needed to be done--so she got it done.

I almost always hit a point in these books where I just don't think it will work, when the hordes of enemies seem too great (for us, the enemies take the form of pesky continuity errors). But then Michael and Steve and Candy and Miha all the JIT readers and all the fans pour their energy into the story, helping Chris and I create something big and wondrous.

It's our own form of magic.

And, like Hannah, when we pull of something like that, I feel like I need to pass out for a week.

Usually I can't do that.

There's always another book to write, another adventure to compose, another diaper to change. But this time, I got my "pass out in the sand" moment.

I finished my draft of *Unlawful Passage* late into the night (technically it was very late into the morning), tossed and turned for a couple hours before giving up on sleep, and packed for a canoe camping trip down the Allegheny River.

I kissed my wife and son goodbye, told the Age of Magic team I was leaving everything in Chris's hands (a terrifying proposition, I assure you), and went on a long weekend.

I spent my days floating down the river, spent my nights drinking around the fire, and then I got a solid 10 hours a night to sleep in the hammock.

In short, it was an awesome vacation.

Which was fun to experience after wrapping *UP*, because this book was sort of a vacation for our characters--at least it was meant to be.

Poor Karl.

As we put the nails in Adrien's coffin, closing the first ROM Arc, and started working on the Lilith Quest, Michael suggested that we first write a smaller, self-contained story (he's always butting in like that and giving us tremendous advice). It gave us, and Team Triple B, a chance to breathe a little bit between saving the city and saving the world. Of course they were going to get into trouble along the way (they're kind of an unruly bunch), but even heroes should get the chance to put their feet up once in awhile.

But the real world calls, and all true Arcadians must answer. We're already cruising through Book 6, which puts our team back on quest AND introduces some drastic changes that will ripple through the Age of Magic as a whole. I think you'll like them.

In the meantime, I hope you enjoyed this little romp along the way.

For the Boulevard,

Lee

Want a free book from Chris and Lee? Sign up for their newsletter and get a copy of The Devil's Due:

https://www.subscribepage.com/chris_and_lee

AUTHOR NOTES - CHRIS RAYMOND
WRITTEN AUGUST 3, 2017

Most of the year I love watching slow, intense movies. You know, the kind most people never hear about and win awards from film festivals in foreign European cities... yeah, those.

What can I say, a man has his tastes. [Edit Michael - *However poor they might be ;-)*]

But when it comes to the summertime, I'm a sucker for getting together with a couple of guys, cracking open a beer or four and enjoying a big action blockbuster. Just the other day, Lee talked me into watching John Wick 1 and 2 back to back. Honestly, he kind of dragged me into it, but once I was settled into a recliner, adult beverage in hand, I revelled in the action that pulled me along scene after scene after butt-kicking scene.

Michael has a philosophy of storytelling that he has sold us on: Life's hard, fiction shouldn't be.

And he's winning me over.

Outside of my writing life, I'm still currently working in education. It's a good gig. A really good gig, but like all work, it has its challenges... budget cuts, bureaucracy, long hours, and piles and piles of grading that *never* seems to go away.

Then comes summertime!

A time for lazy mornings, big action movies, vacation, long nights around the fire, and laughing with my kids until we're ready to throw up. It's the pressure valve in education. A time to just cut loose. It's a time to recharge and not worry about the grind.

We want the Age of Magic to feel like summertime, every time you start a new book!

As we work with all of the authors in the Age of Magic, it has been a freaking blast to help lean them away from building extended tension to being playful, even when things are tough. The series are filled with exciting adventures, but also tons of laughs. If you haven't yet, you should check out the other series in the AOM.

After the first arc, we needed something like this. A pivot between the Battle for Arcadia and Hannah and her friends quest to save the freaking world! We needed just a fun romp, and I think (hope) that's exactly what we wrote.

Let me just say, writing Hannah and her friends are nearly as fun as reading them. I'm falling in love with these characters, and, as they grow together as individuals and a team, I can imagine exactly what they are going to become… one dick joke at a time.

Thanks for coming along for the ride!

Cheers,

Chris

PS, Speaking of playfulness, my daughter, Simone, got into a school for the performing arts. She's the real artist in the family! Nothing brings her more joy than creating.

She specializes in drama and music... but also dabbles in film. Did I mention she's 12?

When she asked what she could do to help give my author career a shove, I made a joke about her creating a video for us. Then Lee and I got to play around, making her stop motion video into something for our fans.

After a few hours of laughing, and way too many takes, we ended up with this!

Enjoy the show.

(My daughter is amazing)

https://youtu.be/eZJ3BMx2xwg

Want a free book from Chris and Lee?
Sign up for their newsletter and get a copy of The Devil's Due:

https://www.subscribepage.com/chris_and_lee

AUTHOR NOTES - MICHAEL ANDERLE

August 3rd, 2017

Dammit!

Ok, let me get this out of the way because it is the MOST important part. THANK YOU! Not only for reading our book, but ALSO reading through these author notes, as well.

Now, back to my *Dammit!*

So, PT Hylton (Storm Chasers, Storm Callers) placed a damned video link before my author notes in our Storm Callers book. Now, freaking CM Raymond (*bastard!*) sticks not only a Video Link, but a Video Link done by his freaking 12-year-old daughter!

(The credits at the end are also hilarious, check them out.)

What a way to block an Author Note you PITA!

My youngest son, Joey (also an author, as is his older brother D'artagnan - Books for Joey Here, Books for D'artagnan Here) used to do video's with Lego's when he was about 11-12 as well.

So, I know how cute they are.

The other day in the Slack group, CM Raymond had kinda

mentioned about having to "up his game" because PT was doing these videos (and then Candy Crum did it after PT and hell, Justin might have gotten into the mix as well, I don't remember.) Anyway, Chris mentioned this upping their game and it wasn't until it was time for me to write these Author Notes that I realized.

He *Author Note* blocked me.

Just like PT Hylton...

I hate them both.

While it has been a while since we have seen a story with Hannah (honestly, it hasn't. It was two months ago (June 2nd) when book 04 was released. We just put out books pretty quickly and … well… shit. I need to get mine released soon! I should stop talking about release dates and stuff.)

Ok, timing on release schedule aside, I was going to mention Chris and Lee's efforts to support authors in the Age of Magic: Justin Sloan, Candy Crum, PT Hylton, Brandon Barr and now Hayley Lawson (Age of Madness.) So, while two months isn't very long between books (they have worked on their other books as well) they ALSO supported another five book releases, and another coming out next week.

Pretty freaking amazing!

A fan mentioned that when I spoke to the type of books in a particular age, it really helped him so let me do it here:

The Second Dark Ages (Post Apocalyptic / Dystopian)

Age of Madness (Horror / Zombie (with laughs…cause it has to have them. Think more Ghostbusters.)

Age of Magic (need I say more?)

Age of Expansion (Space Opera, Military Sci-Fi)

We have some 'non' Age specific books coming in the future, as well.

Finally, I'm going to reveal what is 'close' to the logo for the new Age of Madness, I hope you like it!

219

Well, if you like horror zombie w/ humor, that is… Because, it's the Kurtherian Gambit… Even when shit is going down, there's *always* a time to laugh.

BOOKS BY MICHAEL ANDERLE

For a complete list of books by Michael Anderle, please visit:

www.lmbpn.com/ma-books/

All LMBPN Audiobooks are Available at Audible.com and iTunes. For a complete list of audiobooks visit:

www.lmbpn.com/audible

CONNECT WITH THE AUTHORS

Receive updates from Oz by registering your holo/ email address here:
ellleighclarke.com

Facebook:
http://www.facebook.com/ellleighclarke/

Michael Anderle Social

Website:
http://kurtherianbooks.com/

Email List:
http://kurtherianbooks.com/email-list/

Facebook Here:
https://www.facebook.com/TheKurtherianGambitBooks/